Cockleshell Bay

By

Pauline K Murfin

After a serious accident, Sarah Waters was forced to change the direction of her life completely. Over a long recuperation battle she was finally healthy again but left floundering at what to do with herself. It was then she found the small village of Cockleshell Bay.

With the support of her parents and new-found friends Alice and Frank who owned the café next door, Sarah would soon find that her seaside life of crafting jewellery from recycling 'au naturel' items washed up on the beach was just the change she needed.

But the day she finds a suspicious package forces Sarah back into the law enforcement world she thought she'd left behind and threatens to change her tranquil existence forever...

Would the seriously handsome local police officer Daniel Summers ruin her idyllic village home or would it bring the vital spark missing from her life? Together they unearth many local secrets in an effort to solve the mystery of the secret package.

Pauline Murfin is a retired mother, with three grown up sons.

Married for forty three years to husband Graham, they live in a remote village in Northumberland. Pauline and her husband Graham moved to a small village which is part of the Kielder Forest in the Northumberland National Park in 1999. Poor health prevented Pauline from working, so she decided to study for a degree with The Open University. "To keep my brain ticking over", after completing her degree and gaining a Bachelor of Science she turns her hand to writing fiction.

"Something I have always wanted to do" says Pauline.

Also by Pauline K Murfin

To Begin Again
Comraich
Dreams Lost Dreams Found
The Silent Connection
When the Flag Flies Again

This book is dedicated to the usual suspects. To the best proof readers a person could have. Thank you, Elizabeth and Blanche, for your continuous diligence in trawling through my raw manuscript in order that I don't make the most enormous gaffs.

To the West of Scotland, which inspires me to write so easily about its
Wonderful villages and seaside coves.

To Graham who continues to be my long suffering technical wiz of a husband, without his help I would not be the proud author of my seventh book.

To Rebecca Renieri for the wonderful cover design.

And finally to Sarah Foster, my wonderful copy editor who has once again tweaked my manuscript sympathetically, allowing each of the characters to come alive.

Chapter 1

Never again would Sarah take for granted the fact that her day would not begin with the smell of traffic fumes, crowds of commuters jostling for pole position at the bus stop or queues at the traffic lights. That her first scent of the day wouldn't be other people's tobacco smoke or the constant stench of overheated bodies in the heat of summer in the city.

Although it had been circumstances out of Sarah's control that were to change her life forever, never a day went by without her feeling gratitude for the radical twist of fate which meant her days now began with the smell of fresh crisp salt air. Winter or summer it made no difference, Sarah's day started with her walk along what she had began to think of as her own private beach. Her own little slice of heaven.

She walked along the beach pulling behind her a battered old child's trailer, a sort of bucket on wheels. Her first job of the day [and who wouldn't envy this?] was to walk the beach after the high tide had ebbed away, out through the horseshoe shaped bay, returning to the ocean for the next few hours, giving Sarah her pick of whatever had drifted onto the shore.

Sometimes there would be old pieces of driftwood, strange coloured rocks, pieces of old rope that had been dumped overboard by a fishing trawler out at sea. In fact Sarah collected anything which she could recycle or remake into something useful.

How fantastic to know that after such a hectic commute to her previous place of work, she now had her peaceful little flat, her shop and her workshop, all of which happened to back onto the beach, right next door to her favourite café, Alice and Frank's, for her usual coffee and sugar rush to set her up for the day.

All this was a world away from her previous life of four years ago, when at this time of day she would be clocking on to begin her first shift of the day as WPC Sarah Waters of the Glasgow Constabulary. Then as either driver or co-driver of the proverbial jam sandwich squad car she would grab a coffee and doughnut on the run and join the throng of the inhabitants of the gritty city.

She had been happy, in control, she loved her job, and a job she had trained for and thought she would always do until the day she retired, or left to become a happily married woman.

How wrong could she have been? In fact in Sarah's case, about as wrong as it could get. On that day she was to take a life changing route, which would take Sarah on such a journey, she never thought she would survive, let alone emerge even stronger, happier and after a very long road to recovery she would become sanguine.

Thank God, she thought for the hundredth time, for her parents and on reflection, there were times when her face burned with embarrassment at how she would lash out at them in temper or grief or sheer blind panic of what was going to become of her life. Through it all they supported her without question; they set aside their own lives and helped Sarah to come to terms with hers.

Blanche and Ralph were in their late sixties, both with a busy social calendar but after Sarah's accident nothing mattered more to them than her welfare. When Sarah recriminated herself saying that they shouldn't have to give up their lives to look after a thirty odd year old woman they constantly reminded her that her happiness was more important than their hobbies.

With the constant roar of the sea and the wind in her face Sarah sucked in a lungful of salty air as though it was an elixir of life which she would never ever tire of, or what it meant to be free again.

Happy? Yes, yes, she was happy, she had long since realised that before her accident she had been on one path of life and now she was on another, and given the choice she knew now this would be her chosen path for life.

Sarah lifted her shoulders and arched her back in an effort to shake off the memories of the past that she had learned to live with and even become stronger through those very experiences, but which still haunted her in some quieter moments.

Coffee time, thought Sarah – coffee and homemade scones with lashings of jam and cream. Her lips began moisten at the thought of her morning treat. She pulled her wagon behind her which was now almost full, up the beach towards her rear gate which opened onto the beach itself.

Entering the café was always a comforting experience, the smell of home baking which pervaded the nostrils before you were even through the door, its cosily decorated seaside theme, and all things beach-like, making the whole experience even more special. The coastal theme even carried on through to the loos with beach hut light pulls and on the walls were artistically drawn striped deck chairs and large brightly coloured umbrellas, all courtesy of Frank, Alice's husband who quite obviously had missed his vocation.

"Well Sarah, did you find a handsome man washed up on the shore?" Asked Alice. She herself was so happily married to Frank that she thought every woman was missing out if they weren't attached. It had become her mission to find Sarah a 'nice chap' as she put it! Alice's pretty, if rather chubby face was slightly pink as usual from the heat of the constantly baking ovens, even at this time of the morning. Her bright multi-coloured hair drooping slightly from the broad hair band she always wore for 'kitchen hygiene' she would tell you proudly.

"Ha, chance would be a fine thing, anyway who says I'm looking?" Replied Sarah. "Leave me alone, you married people are all the same, you've been smitten so you want everyone else to be."

"Don't get me wrong I love having you as a friend and neighbour, but what possessed you to bury yourself in Cockleshell Bay for goodness sake?" Shot back Alice. "Fine if you're married like me, but unless you find a suitable mate at the Bay [hotel] or even more unlikely, one of your customers, how are you ever going to find a fella?

"I mean it's not as though you look like me… The original Pillsbury Doughboy," Alice continued, "You've got a figure to die for, gorgeous hair although a few colours wouldn't go amiss, and you're tall… Oh so tall… What I wouldn't give for an extra few inches, that's what's wrong with me of course, I'm to short for my weight…but you… Wow all that leg length!"

"Will you give up and stop panicking because I'm not. I've been engaged before and it's not all it's cracked up to be."

With a brief glance around the half empty café, making sure there were no tender children's ears listening, Sarah said to Alice, "With the exception of your Frank, most men have difficulty keeping their trousers zipped… So no thank you, I'm very happy with my life, so just give me my usual which gives me just as much pleasure as any man would."

"Rubbish!" Laughed Alice. "I know I'm a good cook, but if you think that is any kind of substitute for sex, then you haven't met the right man yet."

In an attempt to change the subject from Alice's favourite topic of attempting to find Sarah a man, to her second favourite topic, which was her own wonderful children, Sarah asked, "Is Elli still enjoying nursery? And how did Sammy's school project turn out? I saw Frank and Sammy trying it out yesterday in the wind, and it has to be a contender for the prize. I haven't seen a kite like that before and it flew perfectly, I don't know who was having the most fun – Sammy or Frank!"

"Big kid, I had to keep reminding him it was meant to be Sammy's project which he was allowed to assist, not take over. And as long as Elli could wear her pink sandals she was happy, I'm surprised you didn't hear her this morning – we had a 'discussion'. I wanted her to wear her blue leather shoes in case it rained but she was having none of it, she must take after Frank." Alice said, tongue in cheek.

The café had such a cosy atmosphere even though it was still early May and most of the customers tended to be locals who felt they were able to join in the banter between the two women at this point. However as the season blossomed the café which was the only place in Cockleshell Bay where you could have breakfast lunch and afternoon tea it would be a positive mad house until late September. Luckily Sarah was usually in for her normal fix long before any holidaymakers were out and about, then on to her own little haven.

Chapter 2

As Sarah left the comfort of Alice and Frank's Café, to open up her own little shop she never tired of the thrill it gave her. She would open the brightly painted shutters on the front windows, and then turn on all the lights on the display cabinets which held her beautifully polished handmade jewellery showing it off to perfection.

The double fronted windows of the little shop were made up of tiny panes of glass with the odd mullion amongst them and which lent the shop a Dickensian quality not unlike that of The Shambles in York.

Considering the age of the shop it was in remarkably good condition and once her father had decorated and put in the extra lighting and lots more sockets, which allowed for all the different types of jewellery to be shown off to its best, the little shop looked quite elegant. The layout inside was unusual and yet it suited Sarah perfectly. A door led from inside the shop onto a dog leg staircase to the tiny flat above, and although it could be better described as slightly larger than a mezzanine with only half a dozen stairs leading into the flat, with no tiring steep flight to climb each evening it couldn't have suited Sarah's needs better had it been designed especially for her.

The flat could not have been more tailor-made and the purchase was completed faster than buying a family car. There was never a moment of doubt in Sarah's mind and during all the months of her recuperation there wasn't a course at the local high school which Sarah hadn't completed. She found she had hidden talents.

She began by enrolling on a course in lapidary, the polishing of stones and rocks, and then joined a jewellery-making course, which led her to expand into silver making. This would enable Sarah to include in her finished articles a really good selection of necklaces, rings, bangles and bracelets.

If the course was on craft and on the ground floor then Sarah took it on and she would throw herself whole-heartedly into it until she had mastered almost every course that was available. By the time she had finished she had been known to be the only woman on the carpentry course, and tried her hand at mosaic making and even wood turning. You name it, she had tried it and did a more than capable job.

The work shop at the rear of the shop had a small hatch so that when Sarah was working at her bench she could easily see anyone who came into the shop without having to stand in the shop all the time. As she sat in her own little world shaping, gluing, sanding or polishing, her mind drifted back to that day. It didn't happen as often now, but sometimes the memory caught her unaware and before she knew it she was right there; back in Glasgow, in the squad car with Stevie Thomson her recently assigned partner at the wheel.

They had given chase to a juvenile known to both Sarah and Stevie as a little obnoxious serial joy rider called Terry. Annoying but no great threat as teenagers went. At first the chase went as predicted, Terry knew the streets well and could disappear like a rat up a drainpipe but eventually he would tire of the chase, go to one of the many cul-de-sacs, dump the vehicle and leg it until the next time and Stevie and Sarah wouldn't be able to prove a thing.

But for some reason this time the chase took on a more sinister tack, Terry was dragging the joyride out and Stevie was becoming more and more angry. His driving becoming more and more reckless in pursuit of what was no more than a kid joyriding which carried no more penalty than a smack on the hand and a fine so why put your life or a member of the public's in danger for nothing.

"Let it go Stevie, he'll probably turn it over anyway, just let him go, we know who he is and we'll get him next time."

"Sod that for a game of soldiers, I'm going to get the little shit if it kills me!" Stevie's voice had an edge to it that Sarah didn't like, his temper seemed barely controlled and he had a look on his face that said he wasn't going to stop the chase until someone was finished. As the chase eventually led into a street that Sarah recognised as being a dead end she was just breathing a sigh of relief at the fact that nobody had been seriously injured in the reckless chase when the youth's car suddenly spun out of control and it was at that point that Stevie's face lit up and with an evil grin he spat out the last words Sarah would hear for a long time.

"Gotcha, you little shit you won't do that again, not to me!"

Sarah's memory of that night was as clear as day, she saw it all in slow motion, the squad car heading straight for Terry in his stolen Ford Fiesta. She could quite clearly see his terrified eyes beneath his baseball cap as the squad car crashed deliberately into the side of the little car.

The windscreen on the squad car shattered like a giant spider's web, in what seemed to Sarah to be complete silence. As the airbags blew up like over blown beach balls, just in time for Sarah's upper body to bounce onto, only to be thrown back against her own headrest. The whole episode she supposed afterwards had only taken a matter of seconds yet until the crash and the bang and the grinding of metal against metal burst through the sound barrier of silence everything else seemed to stand still.

Chapter 3

Waking up in a horizontal position in what felt like a vice with only the glare of a strip light on the ceiling, had to have been more terrifying than any villain Sarah had ever encountered in her job. Yet here she was her heart pounding before she could get a word to escape from her dry lips.

"Where am I? Hello, hello is there anyone there?"

"We're here darling, we're here, you're in hospital, don't try to move, you'll be alright… I'll go and get the Doctor; we've been waiting for you to wake up… Don't worry, Dad's here, he'll sit with you while I go and get the Doctor…"

Blanche's voice was urgent, unsure, upset, but relieved that her daughter had spoken. Oh thank God she thought. Her daughter had spoken and she's alive, she kept thinking to herself, thank God for that. As she hurried through the closed curtains which hung around the bed in an attempt to allow privacy for patient and Doctor yet everyone knew what was going on behind the makeshift walls.

Sarah felt a strong hand tighten around her fingers and suddenly that small gesture gave her comfort, she wasn't alone.

"Hi… my little girl, we thought you were never going to wake up. You've had an accident in your car, but you're going to be alright. And you haven't got to worry because your mum and I are going to look after you and you will come and stay with us until you are back on your… Well, until you feel well enough."

"Dad, Dad, I'm confused, tell me, please, why am I in this collar thing, have I hurt my neck? Is it whiplash? I'd love to sit up and I really would love a drink of water please."

"Don't worry I'll get you a drink as soon as the nurse comes, and when the Doctor comes he'll explain why you have the collar on, but please don't try to move in the meantime, I know it's difficult for you take it all in but everything will be fine I promise."

But everything wasn't fine, the Doctor was later to tell Sarah, she had broken her back in two places and they had operated placing two steel rods into her back, which held her damaged spine together. They told her how she had been extremely lucky and that a centimetre to the right or left and she would have been paralysed so in their opinion she would still be able to carry on a full and healthy life.

Sarah would never forget the way in which she had been told that life as she knew it was over for her, but that she should be grateful that it hadn't been worse. That she could still lead a 'full and active life'. They gave her a shiny new wheelchair which they said she would soon get the hang of, but first she would have some excruciating physiotherapy… all in a good cause they told her if she complained, 'no pain no gain' she was told until she wanted to scream.

Then her Mum and Dad tentatively suggested that… only temporarily, she should come to stay with them. Sarah wanted to refuse, complain she needed her own space, but it made no sense, she was just being stubborn. She knew she was being a pain but some days she simply couldn't help herself but it was obvious to everyone that her upstairs flat was never going to be an option until she was on her feet again… and this was something Sarah repeated like a mantra.

As if the accident and all its physical problems wasn't enough there was the ongoing investigation into the reason for the accident.

All Sarah wanted to do was concentrate on getting back on her feet again, she was entitled to use the police gym facilities and she had a couple of times, until she began to feel a bit like an injured army vet. It was as though she were another species, as though she was no longer a member of the team, but an injured outsider.

Ralph was wonderful even if Sarah didn't fully appreciate it at the time. He would take her to the physio unit at the hospital, sit and wait in the café while Sarah put herself through hell. No amount of persuasion from the staff or Doctors could make Sarah slow her pace, and her pain could be clearly seen etched on her contorted face. She was relentless in her pursuit of being able to walk again and back to work, putting this whole nightmare behind her.

It soon became apparent that after the initial flow of good wishes flowers and cards from her colleagues, that life went on without her and so did the job. She had heard that Stevie who had come out of the crash unscathed had been assigned another partner. He hadn't even had the good grace to visit her, although her Mum and Dad said he did come to the hospital when she was unconscious. Her father hadn't been enamoured with him, had called him a 'wideboy' in his opinion.

That was until the day he had turned up at her parent's bungalow holding a bunch of flowers and a basket of fruit. Sarah would never forget that day, she felt as though she had been threatened by the Mafia. He had told her that if she didn't uphold his version of events her life would be over, not only in the police force but socially too. Oh he didn't come right out with it, he made a little small talk first, gave his usual 'knock the girls' socks off' smile but which didn't quite reach his eyes, before delivering the killer blow with that sickly sly grin on his face. Apparently everyone at the station had completely accepted that Terry had been at fault and that he, Stevie, had had no choice but to run into him. It was unfortunate, he went on delivering his version of events as a fait acompli, that she had been injured in the process but it was Terry's fault. He was the toerag who had stolen the car, wouldn't stop when asked and he, who had caused the accident.

When Sarah told him to take his flowers and fruit and bugger off out of her parents house and that she would see him at the hearing, where she would tell her version of events he had laughed menacingly, bending down to the level of her in her wheelchair leaning over her until she could feel his garlic scented breath on her cheek as he delivered his final words.

"Try it, Waters and you're dead, no miserable cripple is going to ruin my career." And then he was gone. Before her accident Sarah could have dealt with most incidents no matter how sticky and not bat an eyelid. She wouldn't have said she was tough or hard, she was still feminine, but she had developed a working shell that helped her to survive in the job without either wetting herself with fear or crying with despair. But a direct threat with the knowledge that he had managed to convince everyone at the station that the accident had played tricks on her mind rendering her account unreliable was almost impossible to fight.

It was almost a year to the day of the hearing, where Sarah's testimony was deemed unreliable due to the severity of her injuries clouding her judgment. She knew she would never be able to return to the job she had loved. Disappointed at the amount of her colleagues who hadn't turned up at the hearing to give her moral support helped Sarah see that to return to the past, to the way things were, was never going to happen even though she was almost there physically, she could stand, she could even walk short distances. Something the Doctors had said couldn't happen. She was sure that given a few more months she would be back on her feet back to… To what, she thought? She knew she could never return to active duty, and she couldn't bear to sit behind a desk all day even if a job were available at her own station. And even then would they want her back? Could she work with those colleagues who hadn't taken her word for the events, the word of their friend and colleague, rather than some slimy git who hadn't been at the station two minutes?

It was at that moment if Sarah only but knew it that her new life was about to begin. She decided after having frank discussions with her Mum and Dad that she would take her redundancy enhanced package which would be quite substantial, she would also put her flat on the market. Although she knew that within a short space of time she would be walking again and could leave the wheelchair behind, she was never going to be able to live in a third floor flat with no lift.

The next couple of months seemed to fly past, once again her parents were brilliant, Ralph and Blanche organised to have her furniture put into storage, helped Sarah trade her own beloved Mazda sports car in for a much more sensible car vehicle with better lumbar support and easier to climb in and out of than a very low sports car. By this time she had almost stopped going to physio as she was now able to walk and it was almost unnoticeable to anyone except the trained eye that Sarah was still in considerable pain if she stood or walked for too long.

It was one night as all three of them sat watching television and for the third time Sarah gave out a huge sigh. It was obvious to both Ralph and Blanche that she was becoming restless, they were afraid for her but knew this sedentary life was not for Sarah. It was Blanche who came up with the idea.

"You remember Mrs Burns, Sarah? You know you went to school with her Carol? Well she's just come back from having a holiday in the most beautiful place. Its erm, now what did they call it… it's on the seaside… Oh erm Cockleshell Bay… in the West you know, it's always lovely and warm in the West. Well anyway she says it was the quaintest little village right on the beach and, well anyway she said it was lovely. I just thought maybe you could take a little break, have a little holiday before you decide what you want to do with your life."

Sarah was about to pooh-pooh the idea, when the theme tune for a well known soap came on the telly, a soap she knew both her Mum and Dad had followed for years and she couldn't stand, so they would quickly turn to a different channel. It suddenly dawned on Sarah how thoughtless she had become, how ungrateful she had been. When she had been in pain or simply feeling bloody minded and sorry for herself, her Mum and Dad had been absolute bricks. They'd just given up their whole lives, their hobbies, their routine and their friends all for her.

They'd had no time to adjust to having their lives disrupted it had just happened, but they hadn't complained. It was only fair, that they should have their own lives back, she wasn't the only one to want things the way they were.

"Does she have a brochure or anything for the place?" Sarah said casually to her Mum after making an instant decision. "What did they call it, Cockleshell Bay? It sounds nice doesn't it, and I'm driving now so there's no reason why I couldn't have a little break. In fact I think that's a wonderful idea Mum."

Blanche and Ralph tried not to look too pleased but it was obvious that not only were they pleased that their Sarah was well enough, after what happened to be able to a holiday independently. But also it had to be said, it would be a relief even for a couple of weeks to flop back into retirement mode and slow the pace down a notch. They never resented a single minute they had spent looking after the love of their life, however as you got older your pace of life slackened and to speed it up overnight into thinking for someone else had been a challenge to say the least.

It just so happened that it was whilst holidaying in Cockleshell Bay that Sarah decided that this was where she wanted to spend the rest of her days, although, as you'll see, the peace and quiet of the seaside location was not always as it seemed.

Chapter 4

To say that Blanche and Ralph were shocked would be an understatement, the day Sarah arrived back to give them the news that she had bought a shop with a flat above it in Cockleshell Bay. She had set the wheels in motion herself with the police pension and Human Resources department.

All of that was almost four years ago, her Mum and Dad had come up trumps once more after their initial shock. They followed Sarah in convoy back to Cockleshell Bay, both cars full to the gunwales with what seemed to Sarah everything from her Dad's decorating department in the garage. Once they had got over the shock and Sarah explained about the living accommodation and the fact that the little shop would bring in an income and it was only a matter of a couple of hours away from both of them, they had warmed to the idea.

They, like Sarah knew that she could never go back to a physical job and after she had taken all those classes it was obvious she had talent, so it made perfect sense to open a little shop. She could afford it and she would even have her police pension to supplement her income if the shop wasn't enough.

"Of course it's the right thing to do," Ralph had assured Blanche when they were lying in bed speaking in whispers the night before they would all travel down to Cockleshell Bay. They didn't want Sarah to overhear them discussing her as though she wasn't capable of making her own choices at her age, however as Blanche pointed out it was less than a year since Sarah was lying in a hospital bed lucky that she wasn't paralysed and in a wheelchair for life.

And yet here she was leaving to start not only a new life but a business as well.

But as soon as her parents saw the little shop and the cosy flat above with its view straight out to sea they were just as blown away as Sarah had been the minute she had viewed it.

All three of them stayed at the Cockleshell Bay Hotel so that they had a comfortable place to eat and sleep while the move took place. In fact, Ralph was in his element decorating as Blanche made the tiny little flat clean and ready for carpets to be fitted and Sarah's furniture to arrive from storage.

Sarah insisted that her Mum and Dad have a sea view room and the bill was to be sent to her. The hotel was run by a couple in their fifties and as Blanche had put it to Sarah the hotel was 'nipping clean'. It was as they were having their breakfast one morning at the hotel before going over to the shop to carry on where they had left off the night before. Sarah took a long look at her parents, and smiled for the first time in weeks, it was as though a black cloud had been lifted from above all of their heads. It was clear they had come to love the little shop and flat as much as she did and they knew she was going to be all right.

By the time Sarah had moved into her new home and business and her parents had returned to their own lives, slightly little less worried, even though they knew Sarah still tired easily and was in great pain from her injuries, they knew that no matter how much they wanted to wrap their daughter in cotton wool they must let her go and let her regain her own identity, just as they must return to their own friends, hobbies and slightly more laidback life style befitting their ages.

It had been agreed with Bob and Celia, the manager and manageress of Cockleshell Bay Hotel that anytime they came back to the hotel they would be given the room with a view, as that had been part of their stay that they had enjoyed more than anything.

They had got on very well with the wonderful friendly couple, and as Sarah's little flat had only one bedroom and in that was her special bed, with the mattress designed for patients with spinal problems and in her Dads opinion 'hard as nails' they were much more comfortable at the Bay.

Life had, for the first time in over a year began to calm down for both Sarah and her parents, and they kept in touch of course by phone. Gradually they began to worry slightly less and rebuild their own social life once again. Just as Sarah had begun a whole new life in Cockleshell Bay. Her by now regular habits were known in the bay; she walked the beach each morning collecting her flotsam and jetsam then went into Alice and Frank's for her early morning treat before starting her day in her workshop stopping only when and if a customer came into the shop.

It was on one such day as she walked along the beach in the distance she heard a dog barking and a voice calling for it to "Come, come on," that she suddenly decided she needed a companion! In fact she had always wanted a dog or a cat when she had been in the force but she always decided against it simply because it wasn't practical when she worked shifts.

As the idea took root she began to think about what type of dog… yes a dog, rather than a cat she thought to herself, cats are nice but they are not such good company she thought. You can't actually speak to a cat; well you could she thought if you ended up like a dotty old maid as she was in danger of being… She laughed at the direction her own thoughts were taking her. She would ask Alice when she called in for her coffee if there was a cat and dog shelter or rescue centre nearby where she could enquire. She didn't want a puppy, she didn't think she could manage all the training and so on, and anyway it would be nice to give a dog a home that may otherwise have to be put to sleep.

Chapter 5

Sarah became Elli and Sammy's friend for life now that she had her border terrier Scamp, whom they not only helped Sarah pick out of the motley group which they had seen at the rescue centre, but they also chose the name.

Although Scamp looked like a puppy; small and wiry, white with a single black patch over one eye, he was actually three years old. He had belonged to a fisherman who had sadly passed away. The old fisherman had lived at the fisherman's mission a little further along the bay and the old chap had apparently taken Scamp onto the beach which was right outside his door every day without fail. It was obvious to everyone that Scamp could quite easily have lived on the beach as he knew it so well. It was also obvious by his affectionate nature that he loved company and especially that of playful children.

The sea and the beach seemed to have an invisible string that tugged at Sarah and Scamp twice or three times a day simply to walk its length. It was on such a walk she thought about her idyllic surroundings, her little shop, and next door to Alice and Frank's Café which was her most favourite place, Alice and her family had befriended her when she needed a friend. Then of course there was Bob, of Bob Todd's Bits & Bobs the little hardware shop, which had the reputation of if they didn't have it, they would get it for you. Although apparently since Bob's wife Mary had passed away it hadn't been quite the same.

Ah well, thought Sarah, we all take pain and grief in different ways, he'll survive, he may not want to but he will. And of course next door to Bob's was the village post office. Ah, where would we all be without the village post office on pension day? Where it would seem the whole of Cockleshell Bay were catching up on all the gossip. Across the road from the post office where everyone spent their weekly pensions, was the general dealer's. Sarah loved the general dealers, it meant she never again [unless of course it was desperately necessary], had to drive into the smelly crowded and incredibly fast flowing traffic of the city. And to be honest the little general dealers had even stocked up on a type of pre-packaged takeaway Chinese, especially for her. They weren't of course quite the same but it helped to quell her townie's addiction to fast food.

And Fat Charlie's Rock Shop which basically sold all things sweet, guaranteed to rot your teeth or pull out your fillings. The tourists loved it of course as he bought all his stock in from the seaside resort suppliers, selling false teeth, sugar dummies and giant lollies galore. Although his shop door was open all year round, you would normally find Charlie sitting watching his horse racing through the open door to the back shop and usually a shout would bring him to the counter.

Then, standing grandly at the top of the hill overlooking the actual bay itself was the Cockleshell Bay Hotel. Built on actual bedrock they say, and an old grate which can be seen along the beach with a rusty iron gate actually runs underneath the hotel, and many years ago, was used by smugglers. Who no doubt would be smuggling rum into the village? Ah happy days thought Sarah; nowadays it wouldn't be rum they would be smuggling.

After that there were three holiday cottages where holiday-makers came and went, except for one, the nerd they called him, lived there. Well he had for the last six months anyway although they said he was only renting. Some sort of computer wiz apparently, thought Sarah, pale and skinny with glasses.

Lastly, the only other place along the bay was the boatyard, run by Bart and Andy, 'wideboys' as her Dad would have called them. Although to be fair Sarah didn't know for sure, they did however have a reputation for having sticky fingers and doubtful sources for their many shiny toys which sat on their forecourt. These ranged from Jet Ski's, dinghies, motor boats you name it if it floated they sold it and a bit like Bob if they didn't have it they could get it for you, at a price of course!

Sarah tried not to think too closely about where and what they sold, that wasn't her job anymore; she was a civilian and happy to be one, although nothing could stop her copper's nose from twitching. However they were nice lads well, especially Andy, Bart was a little on the rougher side since his father had passed away but Sarah was sure they weren't bad lads at heart just a bit, 'wide' to coin her Dad's description.

Calling for Scamp she suddenly felt the last piece of the jigsaw had fallen into place as she remembered the day she had heard a voice call for their dog and now she was the one calling. And if she ignored Alice's constant matchmaking ideas of how to find her a suitable mate, Sarah could honestly say, she was happy.

If someone had told her a little over four years ago as she sped through the streets of Glasgow, going from one crisis to another and loving every moment of it that she would be more than content, and actually happy, walking the beach in a tiny little village called Cockleshell Bay she would have said "in your dreams". And yet here she was and she was actually living the dream… yes… yes, she was happy and no she didn't rule out the possibility that at some point, in the future, but not now she told herself firmly, she may think of taking another person into her life. But for the present Sarah Waters was happy and after the trauma of not only her accident but also the actions of her so-called friends and colleagues, it said a lot that she could say those words and believe them.

Chapter 6

The Manager and Manageress of the Cockleshell Bay Hotel, Bob and Celia, enjoyed Ralph and Blanche's company so much, that now when they came down to visit their daughter they were automatically given the same sea view room that they had so enjoyed on their first visit. In fact they got on so well with Bob and Celia that they played a mean game of dominos or whist between the four of them.

As the summer heat intensified the bay seemed to shimmer with the humidity, so much so that Sarah's walks along the beach were a welcome break from the sometimes suffocating heat of the shop. It was as she returned from her morning walk she spied Alice sitting out in the fresh air at one of her bistro tables which Frank had bought at the end of season sale from the garden centre last year. She was fanning her plump pink face with the menu card from the table, her sandals kicked off so she could cool her feet on the pavement, eyes closed although she heard Scamp's panting and had already put out a bowl of water for any passing 'hot dog' so to speak.

"God we need some rain," She said without even opening her eyes, knowing exactly whom she was speaking to.

"I'm sure it wasn't as hot as this last year."

"You've said that every year since you've moved here Sarah, and yes it was definitely as hot as this but you're right – we do need a storm to get rid of this humidity."

Summer visitors of course never complained about the heat, after all, that's what they hoped for when they came to the seaside. The following day was a strange day but a welcome relief, a slight breeze started early in the morning as the odd crisp packet fluttered past the window of Sarah's shop, then as the day went on the heavy metal sign from the Bay Hotel began to swing back and forth in the wind then each of the little shops' advertising sandwich boards were gradually removed from the pavement entirely, after having picked them up for the hundredth time.

Alice decided to take her new tables and chairs in as they kept tipping over and she was afraid the glass tables would get broken. By tea time the wind was so strong from further along the bay you could hear the rigging from the boats in the harbour clanging constantly and the seagulls screamed unnervingly on the roof tops. As Sarah went for her evening walk the sand was whipping round the small beach like a sand storm in the Sahara and she was glad to get back indoors.

As the night progressed the wind had revved itself up to gale force and that's when it became worrying. Sarah worried about her roof and her chimney pot. After all, the building was old and since she had been there she hadn't had any major work done on it, presuming the surveyor would have told her if there had been anything which needed immediate attention.

Looking out through her telescope that she kept fixed on the windowsill, Sarah could see as the daylight gradually disappeared and dusk turned to dark. The sea was rough and the waves high, she heard them crashing on the small bay behind her and only a matter of yards away from her little picket fence.

After almost scaring herself to death thinking her roof or certainly her chimney pot was about to fly off or worse still, drop through the bedroom ceiling, she decided to simply go to bed and hope for the best. Sarah had never heard a storm like it, as it raged on and on, becoming even louder and louder, she strained her ears every time she heard a thump or a crash. Positive that she wouldn't get any sleep that night, the tide suddenly turned and Sarah was sure the wind seemed to ease and the torrential rain began. Now that, Sarah thought, I don't mind. In fact she actually loved to be all snuggled up in her bed when it rained she somehow felt secure and eventually drifted off into a peaceful slumber.

As the watery sun of the next morning shone through her bedroom window Sarah woke surprised at the feeling she had actually had a decent sleep considering all the chaos which had gone on the night before, and with a feeling of relief that there was no chimney pot on her bedroom floor she got up and stepped into the shower.

As Sarah and Scamp began their morning walk she was always a little excited especially if it had been a rough sea as to what may have drifted ashore. This morning she had no doubt she would find some interesting things to recycle, the first thing she came across was a lobster pot which had obviously come adrift in the rough sea, and which would make a lovely window decoration just as it was. Then she came across an old orange box and on closer inspection the stencilled writing on the side of it said that its country of origin was South Africa.

"Can you believe that," Sarah said to herself, although she knew it was more likely some chef had thrown it overboard from a liner out to sea, but it still came from the other side of the world and washed up on her little beach. She picked up some rather nice coloured rocks which would polish into nice jewellery. It was as she was examining a particularly nice coloured rock that she could hear Scamp barking and barking and making such a fuss, he loved to find things. She was sure that the old fisherman who had had Scamp from a puppy must have walked the beach outside the fisherman's mission as Scamp had taken to beach combing like a duck to water.

"I'm coming, I'm coming, hold your horses," Sarah shouted to Scamp and she gradually pulled her trailer towards where he was pawing at what looked like a pile of seaweed. On closer inspection Sarah could see it was a plastic bag all taped up. Disentangling it from the clump of wet seaweed Sarah could see it was more like a package than an old carrier bag and it had been taped so much it would be impossible to see what was inside until she cut it free with a craft knife. She threw the parcel into her trailer and carried on along the beach until she had collected every little piece of drift wood. Some of which would make corner shelves which would literally be sold all rough and smelling of the sea. She had found that tourists from the city loved the 'au naturel' feel of these holiday souvenirs.

There were times when Sarah caught herself thinking of tourists as city dwellers and she had to remind herself that only a matter of years ago that's what she was herself. Although hard to believe she often had to pinch herself to know that this was real, this was her life now and she couldn't be happier and if

she had the chance now, to go back…
she would choose not to in a heart beat.

Making her way back to the café for her
breakfast and early morning gossip from
the morning regulars, she knew the talk
this morning would be about the
previous night's storm. Sarah dumped
her trailer in the garden then went onto
the café. After all the regulars had talked
about lost slates and damaged chimney
pots Sarah said her cheerio's and went to
open her own shop.

It was midday when she was about to
take her trailer along the beach again
with Scamp she realised she had emptied
the trailer of her treasures but had thrown
the taped up bag onto the bench to leave
until she was going to cut it open as there
was no way she was going to try to
unpick the thick tape which was securing
it. As Sarah reached for her craft knife
something about this parcel began to

sound alarm bells in her head, why on earth would someone secure something in such a lot of tape unless they wanted it to be waterproof?

She would never know why but she decided instead of cutting it open she would just poke a little hole in it and see if anything came out.

"Ohh no, ohhh no, no, no, I don't bloody believe this. Not here not now… oh bloody hell!"

As a trickle of powder came out of the hole which Sarah had made, like salt from a celler she licked her finger then touched it to the substance, although there was no doubt in her mind exactly what it was before she even tasted it. As Sarah spat out the foul stuff and swore a stream of profanities.

"I don't bloody believe this, why me? why here? No, no, no it'll ruin everything. This is my home; I don't want the bloody circus which will follow the minute I turn this in."

For a single heart stopping moment Sarah almost persuaded herself not to turn it in, to throw it back into the sea where it came from. But the problem is with drugs and especially this quantity which she could hardly comprehend herself, was that drugs brought not only trouble but serious evil. Someone somewhere would be looking for this, and Sarah knew she had no choice but to turn it in. As her mind began to think like a policewoman she knew that with in minutes of handing it in the place would be full of suspicious police, drug squad and sniffer dogs.

And then with a loud groan out loud Sarah thought, of course it would come out that she herself had been in the force, no one would ever think of her the same again. "Once a copper, always a copper," they would say. People would stop talking to her in the same way. She had seen so many times when she had been in the job, that's why most coppers marry other coppers or nurses just as a slight variation for the men.

Sarah wanted to scream, why now? When my life is going so well for God's sake?

It was no good she knew what had to be done and the sooner it was done the sooner it would be over and she could get back to normal. She decided to close the shop and go and get changed, she looked on the internet and found the nearest police station which was in the next village actually and was probably no more than a police house with one copper.

Sarah had got so used to slopping along the beach in her cut offs and flip flops actually dressing to go out of the village was unusual. She had acquired a beautiful natural golden colour from the warm breezes and constant walking on the beach and her hair which was already fair had bleached in the sun and considering she never wore any make up her colleagues from the force would have been very envious at how stunning she looked without even being aware of it herself.

She dressed in cream linen pants with a matching scoop neck tunic top, slashed at the sides showing off her slim waist and which also showed off the glow on her skin to perfection. Then with a simple pair of gold sandals on her feet to complete the outfit, she had no idea how stunning she looked. Bringing her little Suzuki Jeep round the front of the shop she was aware of Alice's curious gaze through the café window and realised this was where the evasive behaviour began.

She had been unable to bring herself to tell Alice about her find in case she [how ridiculous!!!] was involved… That's what being a policewoman did to you, you trusted no one, and she hated that about the job.

She found the village where the police house was and her directions took her to the very top of the hill where a large white house overlooked the bay below. As she parked the car and stopped for a moment to gather her thoughts she took a look at the spectacular view of the bay where she could see her own village in the distance.

The sign told her this was the local Police Constabulary and another sign clearly indicated the office, which was attached to the side of the house. She gave a heavy rap on the door, actually it was probably much heavier than she had intended but once she had made up her mind to do it she had taken a deep breath then dropped the knocker. However, after waiting and knocking several times it was quite clear there was no one in.

This was rather strange as the police's four wheel drive was parked at a jaunty angle on the sloping hill. Just about to return to her own vehicle, she heard a voice call, "I'm coming, sorry won't be a minute…"

The voice came from somewhere around the corner and Sarah's curiosity took her to see who was calling. Nothing could have prepared Sarah for what she saw as she popped her head round the corner. Alice would have positively drooled, had she been here, Sarah knew that.

Sarah's first view of this bronzed Adonis was his back and if his front was as good as his back he must be absolutely gorgeous. And she wasn't disappointed, as she coughed in order to let him know she was behind him, this six foot guy dressed only in boxer shorts swung round. He had the most gorgeous smile showing off his whiter than white teeth set in his very tanned face and Sarah had to stop herself staring like a dumb struck teenager.

This vision of manhood was attempting to hang a wetsuit over his washing line which he had quite obviously only minutes before been wearing. With his whiter than white toothpaste smile he apologised for his attire but explained he wasn't actually on duty today, however he would certainly help if he could?

Chapter 7

When Sarah managed to drag her mind back to the business in hand she coughed in order to clear her throat as she prepared to blow this local copper's mind.

"Hi my name is Sarah Waters, I have the jewellery shop in Cockleshell Bay."

"Hi, how can I help you Ms Waters? I'm Daniel Summers, area sergeant in charge of the county."

He had a gorgeous smile which Sarah knew she was about to wipe from his lovely face in a matter of minutes. Then the whole atmosphere would go from something akin to enquiring about a stray dog, to drugs, trafficking and contraband. And certainly no time off until the big wigs went back to whence they came.

Sarah lifted the package from her bag and peeled off the little piece of sticky tape she had placed on the hole she had made while investigating.

"I should explain that I understand what this is, only because until fairly recently, I myself was in the police force until I left through injury. So in my opinion this is heroin."

Daniel took the package from Sarah's hand and did exactly what she had done, licking his finger and tasting the substance then spitting it out.

"Wow, your dead right about it being heroin, where on earth did you find this?"

"Well as I mentioned I have the jewellery shop in Cockleshell Bay and I use a lot of what I find on the beach and recycle things such as rocks or drift wood. Well as you'll remember last night we had an horrendous storm and this is what I found first thing. I did find one other thing but I suppose it could just be coincidence but it could also be connected. I found an old lobster pot which I presume had broke loose from its buoy. The package may have been anchored to that, but I'm only guessing. Anyway it's your responsibility now."

Sarah turned to go greatly relieved that her part was over now, but Daniel who saw just as clearly as she did that as soon as he told the relevant authorities about this hot potato things were going to get very lively around here. And he, like Sarah, really didn't want that – he liked his life exactly as it was with the odd theft of diesel from the local garage, missing cats and dogs and of course the McFarlan brothers' sticky fingers.

"Hey what's your hurry, would you like a coffee while I take some details?"

"What details do you need, you know my name and where I live and now you have the package – that lets me out."

"And me in. Oh, I get it." Daniel gave her a wry smile that told Sarah all she needed to know and actually she did feel a bit sorry for him. After all she had had a couple of hours to get used to the fact that finding the damned parcel was going to change everything for a while. Whereas he had just had it dumped in his lap before he'd hardly taken off his wetsuit, and that would mean there would be no more leisure time for him for a while.

Sarah looked over towards the fabulous view of the bay where he had placed an old wooden table and chairs, presumably

to eat alfresco on such a beautiful
evening.

"Well if your offer for coffee still stands
then, thank you that would be very nice."

Sarah smiled at Daniel and couldn't
possibly know how it had made his heart
race. His first thought was, why hadn't
he met her before now, why now when
their world was about to be turned upside
down by the pretentious overbearing
heavies of the drug squad? Minutes later
they sat drinking their coffee at the table
which was perched high on the hill,
giving the most amazing view as the sun
shimmered on the ocean and the breeze
was just enough to keep you cool, and
neither one wanted to spoil the moment
by broaching the subject of the parcel.

"You know for two pins I'd throw this
into the sea, you realise this is going to

ruin the summer for us both when the heavy squad get here?"

"Ha, Sergeant tut, tut, how dare you, you are a man of the law, but don't think I didn't think exactly the same as you. However we both know that drugs brings trouble and someone somewhere is looking for this and sooner or later it would come back to bite us.

"Listen," Sarah spoke, more urgently than before. "I came here to get away from the big city and away from the force and some of the seedier characters. The last thing I wanted was to find a parcel worth God knows what, it must be in the millions of pounds worth of dope on my little beach.

"And… Well to be honest … and don't get me wrong and I don't mean to hurt your feelings but I haven't actually told anyone I was in the force before. Well…

You know how it is, nobody trusts you, no one talks to you the same, and they start watching everything they say… You know, you must know, it must happen to you?"

"Well, I do know what you mean," replied Daniel, "but I have earned the respect of the locals and they also know I'm not ticket happy and I don't go round deliberately looking for trouble. I have established a presence so they know we have law and order but then I tend to keep a low profile.

"I have found that works and I'm sure that when you've been here a while… how long have you been here by the way? I haven't seen you before although I did see the shop had been taken but didn't know by whom?"

"I've been here four years and I live in the flat above the shop, as I say I make jewellery and different craft items and I do very well."

"I wouldn't have thought you would have done enough business to make it worth your while?"

"Well to be honest I do more internet sales than I had ever imagined, so the shop is a bonus and where my workshops are."

"And you don't get bored after living in the city? Which city by the way where were you in the force?"

"Glasgow for my sins, and no I definitely do not get bored, I love it here."

"Well as much as I am really enjoying your company and I only wish the circumstances were better, I suppose I can't put it off any longer, I'll have to let the drugs squad know about your find. So you can expect a visit from them and no doubt customs and Uncle Tom cobbly and all. But I'll be in touch and keep you posted if I can before they get here, and it's been nice to meet you… Sarah? Er.. very nice."

"Yes, me too… Daniel?"

Sarah shook Daniel's outstretched hand returning his smile, with the first genuine smile towards a person of the opposite sex in well over four years, and meant it – and she also got the feeling that perhaps he did too.

Chapter 8

As Sarah pulled away she sneaked a look in her driving mirror and she could quite clearly see Daniel watching her retreating vehicle. If she wasn't mistaken, he had a look that said he found her as interesting as she had found him.

Suddenly her mood lifted and she certainly felt a lot better than she had driving up the hill, with what felt like a bomb in her bag. Now she felt as though not only had she passed the buck but that in some way she had gained an ally in the fact that neither one of them was very chuffed about the fact that some stupid smuggler had managed to upset other people's lives, how inconvenient of them, thought Sarah with a giggle to herself.

The sun was still warm when she arrived back in the village as the breeze gently blew off the land and Sarah couldn't wait to kick off her sandals and feel the sand between her toes. She opened the door for Scamp who came bounding out running straight onto the beach and into the gently lapping waves. Sarah knew how he felt; it was such a beautiful evening she didn't even stop to change out of her good clothes. As she walked she couldn't help but recall her conversation with Daniel… Daniel… he was really nice looking, thought Sarah. "Who am I kidding," She said out loud, "he was gorgeous!"

As she wandered she began to relax for the first time since she had found the incriminating parcel, Sarah suddenly stopped, sure she could hear music. In fact she was positive this time, she had thought she had heard it before, but only at certain times, actually it was when the wind was in the right direction.

She wouldn't dare tell Alice or she would really think she was turning into some nutty old maid beachcomber. But she was sure it was trumpet music, yes she was sure, it sounded like a record her Dad used to play, an old record on Sunday mornings while he peeled the potatoes for her Mum… now what was it she thought frantically… Clavert…. Eddie Calvert, her Dad used to say.. The man with the golden trumpet… that's it… She even thought she recognised a few bars of the song that she could hear… It was something like… erm, 'Oh My Papa' or something like that. She remembered it because her Dad used to play it loud enough to break the sound barrier when you were trying to have a lie in on your day off which was very annoying and rather unforgettable.

Then just as it had come it went and even if Sarah strained her ears for the haunting sound she couldn't hear it anymore. Giving herself a mental shake and explaining the plaintive sounds as some distant record player she carried on her walk.

The following morning, while busy working in the back shop soldering a piece of fine silver, Sarah heard the shop bell ding signalling a customer. She laid down the soldering iron very carefully on the rest and began to remove her safety glasses, when she looked through the hatch and on through the shop window, there parked outside she could see the very familiar blue and yellow check of a police vehicle.

"Damn, here we go," Sarah thought as she walked through into the little shop then suddenly from behind one of the jewellery cabinets appeared Daniel. He looked a lot different to their first encounter, in his black short sleeved uniform, his weapons belt synching his slim waist and holding his flat cap in his hand he did however still have his ready smile.

"Oh it's you?" She stammered, a little taken back,

"Well good morning to you too Sarah, I have had nicer greetings but to be fair not many that look as nice as you," grinned Daniel.

"Flatterer!" Sarah smiled and apologised for her greeting.
"Sorry – to be honest I thought it was the circus and although I worked in the force and have nothing to be worried about, this whole thing has unnerved me a little. You know what the drug squad are like; a bunch of d– heads… Oops sorry!"

"No I totally agree with you and the last thing we need in Cockleshell Bay is a whole load of townies upsetting everyone. But I thought I better let you know they will be here sometime this morning, actually probably in the next hour or so."

"Well that's very kind of you Mr Village bobby, ha ha not many of those about anymore are there? Listen I need to ask you something."

"Go ahead, respectful member of the public… not many of those about nowadays either, ha ha."

"It's a little difficult as I know everyone is under suspicion for the responsibility of the drug package, which is obviously part of a smuggling operation. However common sense tells me that simple people such as my friend next door who owns the café is your typical married woman with two children is not in the least involved. And my dilemma is... My friend is absolutely lovely, fabulous, and honest as the day's long, however she likes to know what's going on and I am going to look like the biggest rotter if she finds out in a few hours that I knew something and didn't tell her first.

"Can I simply give her the low down so that she feels as though she had the original scoop direct from the horse's mouth as it were? Also the minute your vehicle pulls away she will break her neck to get in here to find out what the hell is going on. Oh and another thing she is determined to find me a date and oh God I never mentioned I had previously been in the force… Oh I hate this, it's going to look as though I've deceived her ever since I arrived and she and Frank have been so wonderful with me ever since I opened the shop." Sarah knew her tongue was running away with her here and she'd admitted more than she had intended but she couldn't help it, and now she'd lost her cool in front Daniel, of all people!

Daniel moved closer and put his hand casually over hers, saying, "Hey listen; I'm sure you're right about the woman not being a suspect, although I must admit there have been a few surprising drug smuggling grannies. But I'm sure in this case you could give her the lowdown in such a way as she feels she has inside information, which only you as an ex copper could tell her. That'll surely take the sting out of you not telling her, you could always let her believe you were some sort of secret agent copper who wasn't allowed to talk about it?"

"Ha, ha," Laughed Sarah, recovering herself somewhat, "Well to be seen you're in the force, as you can create an alibi in ten seconds flat, you're good, you're very good."

"Oh and as for that date she is trying to find you? Well I wouldn't mind helping out there either?" Daniel gave his big white perfect teeth smile before giving a slight wink of the eye and as he made towards the door he put his cap on his head leading Sarah to get that rush of warmth she felt when she saw a handsome guy in uniform… And this time this guy also seemed to be 'nice,' let's hope her instincts were right this time.

Daniel climbed into his four wheel drive and this time it was Sarah who was staring after the retreating vehicle with a smile on her face and look of interest in the occupant.

Chapter 9

Sarah began to count to ten but actually only got to three before the shop bell dinged and in burst Alice, even pinker than usual with curiosity.

"Ok what's happening? What's going on? And what's with the disappearing act before closing time last night and a visit from PC Plod this morning.. Although he did look rather tasty... but that's beside the point."

"Ok, OK listen I shouldn't really tell anyone this, but," Began Sarah, leaning closer to Alice and speaking in a conspirital tone so that Alice would feel like she was being given privileged information.

"After the storm the other day I found a package on the beach…. And well not to put too fine a point on it, it was full of heroin. And I know this because…. and you mustn't tell anyone this… I used to–"

"Be a drug addict.. er ..a dealer… a.."

"No, I was not a druggy or a dealer!" Said Sarah, in an affronted tone of voice. "Actually I was in the police force myself, however I left after an accident and now I'm just Sarah… retired… jeweller... and beach comber, Ok?

"I had to take the parcel to the local constabulary," Sarah continued, "Which as it happens is in Lady Bank just up the road last night that's where I went. And I'm sorry I couldn't tell you about it until now as its all a bit hush hush. I told Daniel that you are my closest friend and I was sure you were not a drug smuggler and that I was going to let you in on the action before the big boys come from the drug squad and customs. Now are you happy?"

"Yes… but oh Sarah, drugs on our beach in our village they must have been anchored off the beach and broke loose in the storm… and what about you being a…. secret police… oh shush… Sorry I won't say another word about it, you can take my word for that it'll be like you've never told me. But hey what about that copper …. Daniel eh, on first name terms then already? And a visit this morning he must have wanted to see you again."

"Alice you are incorrigible! It was business, and I know his name is Daniel because he introduced himself that's all."

"And am I? Your closest friend? Don't worry, mums the word about what you were… you're just Sarah the lonely old maid who walks the beach in search of a man... OK?"

"Out you, get back to your customers…. And Alice, thank you."

"For what?" Asked Alice as she made to go out of the door.

"For being you, and because I thought you would treat me differently when you found out I'd been a copper, but that really was in a different life, one which I'll never go back to. I love being simply Sarah the beachcomber of Cockleshell Bay."

Chapter 10

Nothing was the same over the following days; the peace and quiet of the village was disrupted completely. Vehicles coming and going and if it hadn't been for Daniel setting an example and parking his vehicle in the Bay's large car park, those pompous know-it-alls from the big smoke would have blocked off the entrance to the beach with their two saloon cars, huge surveillance van, and smaller van for the sniffer dogs.

Sarah was surprised but pleased that no one had arrived to question her. Alice on the other hand, would loved to have been questioned. The café didn't suffer either as they sold more bacon butties than ever before, coupled with gallons of coffee and tea. Alice was in her element every time a group of officers came she would ask them straight out if they were 'plain clothes' or 'undercover cops', always keeping an eye open for any single attractive males which she could possibly team her best friend up with.

For the first time since Sarah had arrived at Cockleshell Bay she didn't walk on the beach, well, not at her usual times. She waited until all of the police were sitting in their vehicles eating and drinking, which they seem to do a lot. To be honest, Sarah wondered what on earth they thought they were going to find, sitting there in full view of any would-be smuggler with half a brain.

Sarah had eventually got her evening walk as they all seemed to have disappeared for the night and hopefully for good, she thought to herself. She breathed in the wonderful fresh salt air which she had missed like a lung full of oxygen. The wind was gentle and as the sun sank slowly down below the horizon, all was right with the world again for the present. Scamp ran like a mad thing possessed after being practically housebound since the invaders had arrived, he ran straight into the water then out again skidding sideways along the wet sand then he had a bit bark at the odd seagull before foraging in the seaweed.

"Don't you dare find anymore parcels; I blame you for all this you know."

"You know what they say about people talking to themselves?"

Oh, Sarah jumped and turned at the same time although she had instantly recognised the warm tones of Daniel's voice.

"It's when you answer yourself you know you're in trouble," They both said in unison before bursting out laughing.

"Hello again," said Sarah. "I haven't seen you around for a day or two, have you been hiding from the circus?"

"Too right I have. What on earth do they expect to find sitting there for everyone to see, then tracking the whole beach with their sniffer dogs as though a smuggler will leave regular parcels of dope. It was a one off, the parcel could have floated and then drifted in on the tide from God knows where after the storm we had. I think I'm beginning to be a bit cynical in my old age, because actually if they had painted signs on their cars and come with their wooden top helmets on they couldn't have advertised more who they were."

"I think you're right you have become cynical, however certainly not from old age."

Again the twinkle in the eye was most disconcerting when added to Daniel's lovely smile. As they walked and talked they suddenly found themselves back at Sarah's back gate.

"I'm hoping you're going to return the favour of coffee?"

Sarah looked at his cheeky expression and decided it wouldn't do any harm to have coffee now would it?

Scamp sat at the back door while Sarah wiped his feet on his own dog towel before racing up the stairs to sit on the windowsill looking out to sea which was his favourite position.

"If I were conducting this investigation," Sarah started, then looked at Daniel' lifted eyebrows but also his indication that she carry on.

"Well, if I was conducting this investigation, I think I would concentrate on vehicle logs from the coast guard, tidal changes, unusual vessels which have been in touch with the coast guard on a regular basis and also I would have had a team of divers checking out the buoys within for example three mile off the coast."

"Well although this is 'classified' to anyone except, ex police women, their best friend who runs the café next door and scamp, I am going to be diving tomorrow. I did tell them that I dived in the Navy before I joined the police and so I am a trained diver. I know this coast and this area and dive regularly and would be in a better position to know if there was anything unusual, more so than a diver they brought it in."

"Well there you are then great minds think alike, and I'm sure you'll agree that if this was a regular drop gone wrong, that's the only place you are going to find any evidence if there is any left as opposed to tramping up and down the beach all day wasting tax payers' money."

"Ohhh you really have fallen out of love with the force haven't you?"

They were sat comfortably, Daniel on the sofa and Sarah on her firmer, specially-bought chair for her back sipping their coffee, Sarah thought for a moment before speaking.

"Well do you know I didn't think I had, it seemed to have happened little bit at a time. First the accident and the way people who you thought were not only your colleagues but your friends treated you differently when you weren't at work 'doing the job'. I was also disappointed at the loyalty of the actual organisation. Don't get me wrong I loved the job and wanted nothing more than to get back to work, but as it became obvious that, that was never going to happen, well not in the conventional sense of policing, I noticed a gap beginning to widen between those who were coppers and those who were not."

"Listen Sarah…" Daniel said in a more serious voice than Sarah had heard him use since she had met him.

"I want to be straight with you, while I enjoy being less officious than some coppers because it suits my way of life, and I like people, I am still a copper and I must admit to checking you out through records. So I've seen the official version of your accident and resulting injuries. When and if you want to tell me your version then I would be more than glad to hear it, but you don't have to tell me or hide anything from me… OK?

Friends? you're not mad at me for looking are you?"

Sarah could see it had been difficult for Daniel to tell her he had actually checked her out and she had to admit she admired his honesty.

"Hey listen if I'd been in your shoes I would have done the same thing… friends."

Daniel actually leaned over and held out his hand to Sarah who took it in hers and as he held it little longer than necessary she lifted her eyes and she could see the twinkle was right back where it belonged in his lovely dark fringed eyes along with his very handsome smile.

"Anyway you're diving tomorrow then and if they don't find anything do you think they'll move the investigation back to the station and take the circus with them?"

"Hopefully, but I'll only be diving if the weather's right, but yes that's the plan."

"Alice will miss them they spend half of their day in the café and she has made more money in a few days than she does in a month from them. But I for one," Sarah stated, "would like my peaceful life back to normal."

"Are you really not just a little bit lonely on your own?"

"Oh God you sound like Alice, no, no, I'm not lonely… well…"

"Ahha, so you are a little bit lonely?"

"Well not so much lonely as I do miss company now and again. My parents come down regularly to visit but…

"So if I was to ask you out for a drink occasionally you may not refuse outright? Even though I'm a copper?"

Sarah looked at Daniel's handsome face and suddenly thought how nice it would be to have him as a companion to chat to. Someone with whom she could actually talk shop with... His shop; not hers but also someone to have a laugh with as he obviously had a good sense of humour.

"No I wouldn't refuse, in fact I would like that very much." She said. Daniel smiled and opened his mouth in response.

Unfortunately Sarah would never know what he was about to say as his radio chose that time to intervene in their conversation with a message for him to attend some incident or other.

"Duty calls I'm afraid, but I'll take you up on that drink... Sarah."

"Yes... It has been nice... call again, erm... Daniel," Sarah said with a slight flush of her cheeks as he gave her what could definitely be interpreted as a 'see you soon' look, and with a flash of that smile once again then he was gone.

Chapter 11

Sarah slept like a log that night, as though not only had a weight been lifted from her shoulders because life as she knew it was hopefully going to be restored, now that the intruders had moved on. There was also something else which made her smile just as she fell off to sleep; the prospect of her next encounter with the lovely and interesting Daniel.

The following morning dawned bright and sunny and the first thing that came to Sarah's mind was that the dive would take place, as looking through her lounge window she could see that the sea was as calm as a millpond. Had it just been herself and Daniel she would have liked to have been there and in on the act so to speak. But she certainly didn't want to be within a mile of the establishment's cockiest crowd, the drug squad.

Showering and dressing quickly so that she could make her way to the beach for her usual walk with Scamp, Sarah realised that her routine had become like a catharsis. It was where she felt calm and where she had ultimately healed her damaged heart. Oh she knew that wasn't the case in real terms, her heart was as tough as old boots but she had been heart sick when she felt rejected by the only people and organisation she had thought she ever wanted to be with; the police force.

As she walked the familiar path along the shore, deep in thought, Sarah realised she simply hadn't known any different, and how many other people out there were the same. If she hadn't been injured and forced to change her life she would never have known that there was a much better life awaiting for her. And now Sarah knew for certain that that was actually the case, she was much happier now and given the opportunity she wouldn't got back.

Sarah had never been sure why she did it but for some reason she decided to go to the general dealers and buy a bottle of wine and one or maybe two of her Chinese temptations. Was it at the back of her mind to invite a certain handsome policeman? The strange thing about living in a village is that even the staff in the general dealers get to know what food you buy and in what quantities so when the young girl on the till said in conversation,
"Hi Sarah, entertaining then?" Sarah's cheeks turned pink, as she mumbled, "Erm… No, just stocking up." However two Chinese meals teamed with a bottle of wine was bound to draw speculation. Sarah could have kicked herself, before she knew it the whole village would be talking about it.

Once out of the shop however Sarah thought to herself, so what… So what if the village were all agog about her social life…? At least that would mean she was having one, which was a novelty in itself, as for the last four years she had had zilch. And as she kept telling herself, she didn't mind and she certainly wasn't lonely and she didn't miss men one little bit… Liar!

Sarah had taken one look at Daniel that day at the top of the hill with his bronzed torso and hip hugging boxers and realised she had the same yearning for a male companion as the next woman. And if she hadn't lost the knack of recognising the signals altogether the twinkle in Daniel's eyes led her to believe he wasn't averse to her either.

Closing her shop at the end of the day and taking her usual walk along the beach with Scamp, Sarah thought this had to be one of the most pleasant parts of her day. Especially when the weather was as it was this evening, warm and sunny without the humidity or sea fret which could make you feel chilly even in high summer.

Sarah couldn't help but wonder what if anything, the dive had uncovered today. She didn't have to wait long to find out as when she returned who should be standing at her front door with a bottle of wine in his hand but Daniel.

Sarah's heart actually skipped a beat. She hadn't realised that it actually happened in real life, and not just in fictional books such as Jane Austen's novelettes. His smile was contagious as was the twinkle in his eye; he would have made a corset busting Mr Darcy in the eighteenth century, thought Sarah, who was no different to a woman of the past. Her heart still lurched as she took in his tanned face and casual image now for the first time dressed in civvies in which he looked equally gorgeous.

"I'm taking you up on your offer of a drink if that's OK?" Said Daniel, holding up his bottle of wine and inclining his head towards her flat in invitation.

"Do you know you've read my thoughts, wine would be lovely? Have you eaten yet?"

"No I haven't had a chance, I did grab a sandwich at lunch time in between dives just to keep my energy levels up, why?"

"Come up and we'll open that bottle while I prepare something."

As they entered the front shop door Sarah told Daniel that when ever the shop door was locked to simply go round the back and the back door was always open unless she was in bed of course and to feel free to just come in. Daniel gave one of his comical wiggle of the eyebrows which was suggestive without saying a word but coming from Daniel was funny and in no way pervie.

"I should actually reprimand you for leaving your door open to the world, however I know what it feels like to move from the city and actually feel so free that I would hazard a guess you don't even put the alarm on your car now, am I right?" Daniel gave a knowing smile. "I remember the feeling well, it takes a long time before you stop putting your alarm on after living in a City such as Glasgow then when you finally succumb to village life you become complacent. There are still villains even in the country; however that's enough of that."

Sarah put the two Chinese meals in the oven to heat while she took two of her long stemmed wine glasses out of the cupboard realising this would be the first time she had actually entertained anyone other than her parents in this flat, or actually since before her accident.

Daniel leaned nonchalantly against the tiny kitchen door frame while Sarah collected the cutlery and table mats for the little table which sat in front of the large picture window looking out to sea. She threw a crisp green salad together and turned the Chinese food out onto plates as Daniel filled their glasses with wine and before long they were sat comfortably at the table with the most perfect sunset that could almost have been pre-arranged for the moment.

After a moment's hesitation on who would speak first, eventually Sarah could wait no longer to ask how the dive had gone.

"Well… Come on what did you find?"

"To be honest, nothing… well nothing significant… the only thing out of the ordinary was… but it could have been there for years. I did notice that attached to one of the buoys that we looked at, was a piece of red rope. But as I say who's to say how long it had been there. We checked the three buoys, which were within a reasonable distance from the shore; we also checked one or two of the lobster markers that the local fisherman had dropped but apart from a couple of lovely lobsters in one of the pots there was nothing obvious."

"Listen I've been thinking," Sarah said. "The thing is, imagine this, supposing that parcel was meant to be picked up the

night of the storm or the night after …
right?"

"Yes I'm with you carry on, Sherlock."

"Well I remembered that the same day as
I picked up the parcel I also picked up a
lobster pot, it's in the work room. Now
just supposing the pot and the parcel
were supposed to sit quite happily there
waiting for someone to come and collect
it. Doesn't that lead you to believe it
must be someone from the village? And
the storm put paid to all that, by
separating the lobster pot from where it
had been secured and the parcel floated
out through the gaping hole which is in
the side of it.?"

"Actually that's not a bad idea, so
what… are you saying do you think this
is a regular thing or a one off?"

"Oh well I don't know about that, to be honest I think we have to look at a couple of things, firstly who regularly goes out fishing? And I don't mean large fishing boats, because if our hypothesis is right, large fishing boats don't drop their lobster pots in the very deep water, it's too hard not only to drop the pots but also to retrieve them. So I think we are looking for a small vessel that goes out to sea on a regular basis that no one would suspect if they were seen… what do you think?"

"I think you must have been a good copper, and I think you're onto something, we really need to speak to the coast guard and see if they have seen anything unusual. Also supposing, this is not a one off, supposing it has been a regular drop and the only reason we have found out is because on this occasion the storm ripped the pot from hits buoy and it washed ashore."

They had vacated the table and Daniel was lounging on the sofa with his feet up and Sarah was ensconced in her large comfortable chair with her feet curled underneath her. Daniel was now onto coffee as he had to drive home but Sarah was making serious inroads into the wine which did wonders for her, giving her the courage to have some healthy banter with someone of the opposite sex, something she had missed in the last four self-imposed years of abstinence.

"Ok so what we need to do is make a list of those people who not only have boats but regularly go out fishing, probably for lobster or crab, which would account for them carrying pots."

"Yes, and who in your opinion as the local bobby are a 'bit dodgy' ha ha, very scientific but you're the best person to know who on your beat is a bit iffy… my

Dad would call a dodgy character a 'wideboy'… he's very old fashioned like that although his instinct is spot on."

"Right, we've also got to decide if we think this was a one-off or a weekly drop or a monthly drop? I hardly think any less than a month would be feasible what do you think?"

"Yes I hardly think it's like Tesco with a weekly drop, no I think we have to work back to say for instance the night before the storm what date was that and work out say a month after.

We could keep a surveillance to see if we can see any movement at that time, I have my telescope as you can see and I spend hours, looking at the passing ships through it. It's really powerful I treated myself when I first came. And of course we would alert the coast guard."

"Well WPC Waters I think you have just about cracked the case, however I think I should revisit you on several occasions for purely surveillance purposes and of course I would bring plenty of sustenance to keep our strength up while we work what do you think?"

"I think that all sounds perfect Sergeant Summers, anything I can do, I feel it's my civic duty to help our boys in blue… or black as it is now."

Sarah was actually a little disappointed when Daniel made moves to go, as she had really enjoyed her night which had flown over without any feelings of discomfort. It was as though she had known him for years and she hoped he felt the same way about her.

"I'll walk down with you; I always take Scamp out for his last run on the beach before bed anyway."

As they got to Daniel's car Scamp made a run for the beach and Sarah turned towards Daniel about to say she had enjoyed her night when to her surprise he leaned towards her and kissed her softly on the cheek. As he drew back she saw the twinkle in his eye.

"Now the whole village will be talking, not only has my car been outside you're house all evening but they all just watched as I kissed you…"

His eyes had the most outrageous glint in them as he climbed inside his vehicle and then that smile which made Sarah's heart go thud. Before driving off into the distance, leaving Sarah to digest his devilish behaviour, had it been for the neighbours or was it something he had wanted to do all evening just as she had wanted him to do.

Chapter 12

The following morning dawned hot and sunny on Cockleshell Bay. Alice could barely wait for Sarah to arrive back from her walk on the beach to get all the gen from her on her late night visitor. Frank knew Alice wouldn't be happy until she found out every little detail from her friend, and so he suggested they had their coffee outside at the bistro tables while he looked after any other customers.

Frank was as lovely as Alice, a little on the chubby side but Sarah could see how Alice would have fallen for him. In his younger days she could imagine he had been quite a catch. He was a great father to Elli and Sammy as well as helping in the café and running his part-time taxi service, which is how they were able to make ends meet, Sarah supposed.

Sarah had barely turned the corner after putting her trailer in the rear garden when Alice pounced.

"Come on before I burst with curiosity, I've been waiting for you, sit down Frank will bring the coffee's now tell me all and don't leave out the juicy bits because I'll know."

"God you would have made a better policewoman than I did, there isn't much to tell."

Alice's snort was loud enough to be heard in the cafe as several heads turned to look outside.

"Alright, alright keep your hair on!" Said Sarah lowering her voice so that the customers inside couldn't hear, and would hopefully loose interest in their conversation.

"Well… As no doubt you saw, Daniel called last night with a bottle of wine and we had a pleasant evening…"

"Come on all of it, I know you bought two Chinese takeaways at the general dealers so you must have had a cosy meal and a drink…Tell all."

"God it's impossible to keep a secret in this village I should have known that girl on the till wouldn't keep her mouth shut. Ok Daniel arrived with a bottle of wine. He hadn't eaten so I offered to make something, we had a pleasant evening chatting and having a drink before he left OK?"

"Before he left indeed, I saw him kiss you and so did half the village I might add, there must have been more to it than that… come on feed the soul Sarah I don't get to be involved in many romances now that I'm an old married lady you know."

"This is the honest truth I swear Officer!"

Just as Sarah was about to go on, as she said the word officer who should pull up along side the table where they sat but Daniel in his four wheel drive and in uniform so obviously on duty. He didn't get out of the vehicle he just rolled down the window and Sarah jumped up to go to the edge of the pavement to talk to him. Daniel gave one of his dazzling smiles in Alice's direction and said good morning to her which seemed to appease her slightly that she wasn't to be left out or ignored.

"Listen I need you to do a little digging for me today if you can, just try to find out if anyone in the village has a small boat or indeed if they seem to either have money worries or on the other hand money to spare. I'm going along to the harbour to see the McFarlane brothers and one or two others and see what I can dig up there. Are you free this evening?"

Sarah replied that she was sure she was, as her social calendar wasn't exactly bulging with things to do.

"Well if its OK with you I'll pick you up at seven thirty, don't eat and I'll make us something, OK?" And then he was gone, just as swiftly as he had arrived. Sarah knew Alice wasn't going to be happy with a basic explanation and so she prepared to be grilled. She also knew that Alice was a better source of information about the locals than she would be as she had lived here all her life and knew everything about everyone so she would be better served bringing her in on what Daniel needed to know.

"Ooh, things are certainly hotting up around here what did handsome hunk want?"

"Listen we can't talk here, have you got five minutes?"

"Yes of course, Frank knows better than to interrupt me when I'm ferreting."

"Come on then into my place and I'll let you in on what's happening before you burst a blood vessel."

Sarah opened the little shop and automatically began to open shutters and switch lights on as she talked.

"The thing is Alice this is very sensitive, and if I really were still in the force I wouldn't be telling you any of this because you would actually be classed as a suspect... However, as I am positive you have nothing to hide and are not the criminal type I could do with your advice or insider knowledge really."

"OK, I'm all ears."

"Well to begin with I really need to know… and don't forget I'm not in the force anymore this is just Daniel and I trying to solve the mystery of the package and that's all… OK?"

Alice nodded.

"Right, just suppose we are going with the theory that there is a possibility that the drugs parcel was meant to be collected by, say, somebody in the village,"

"What, you're kidding?"

"Well just go with us for a minute, in you're opinion of the locals in this part of the village is there for instance anyone who either needs more money or could be tempted or appears to have more money than they can account for?"

"Emm... listen, Sarah, err just in case there's any kind of investigation I better tell you now… that if it came to income and things, well Frank and me, well we might have been a little creative in our tax assessment… what I mean is Frank doesn't always declare his cash fares for the taxi…"

"We don't make a lot in the café, it's not as though it's bursting at the seams, with customers. To be honest we've made more money since you found the package and we've had coppers crawling all over… But that's all I swear, that's all.

"Alice, neither Daniel nor I are interested in your tax, and to be honest who isn't a little creative with their tax returns. And

I say again, I am not here to snoop, I am not a copper but if we don't get to the bottom of this then the big boys will come back and although it will probably help the sales of tea and scones in your café it will spoil our tranquil village for evermore. So, let's get back to who else we have then, let's go up one side of the village and down the other OK?"

"OK, wow this is fun, better than the excitement I normally have as a wife and mother nowadays. Well as you know next to me is Bob of Bits and Bobs, well he certainly doesn't need any money nor has he been flashing any extra no to be honest there's nothing fishy about Bob. The only thing that was a little… Well how can I put it, suss– but it's not important."

"No Alice you never know in an investigation what is or isn't important, so please tell me."

"Well, Bob loved Mary his wife, he idolised her and when she was ill with cancer he nursed her through the most horrendous pain and it was well known she wanted to die. Well I did hear a rumour that Bob may have helped her along a little… but that's got nothing to do with this."

No you're right, I can't see any connection and if there were any irregularities his motive was born out of love and compassion. No that's nothing to do with us. Who's next?"

"Well the post office, but to be honest the only thing I can imagine Mr and Mrs Veach being involved in is creating gossip and scandal. Although it wouldn't surprise me if the reason they heard about the scandal first hand was that they were guilty of steaming open the mail…

but that's only guess work so no I don't think so… Do you?"

"Well, there's the general dealer, but apart from the fact that they are daylight robbers with the prices, again I don't think so do you?"

"No to be honest, I think we can rule them out, then who else have we got, oh the rock shop."

"Oh Fat Charlie's, no the only thing Charlie is guilty of is running a book… you know taking bets."

"You mean he actually runs bookies from his shop and I didn't know, I thought he just sold rock!"

"God I really am out of practice as a copper, well again to be honest it's not what we're looking for."

"And after all," Said Sarah, "He only runs it because if you want to place a bet you would have to go into the town and it's a long way for the oldies just to place a bet on the national or some such race and he's not doing any harm."

"Then there's the hotel, with Bob and Celia. Did you know that the grate that opens onto the beach runs all the way under the rock itself and into the cellars of the hotel?"

"I've seen the rusty old gate and I assumed it had been used by smugglers in possibly the eighteenth century or there abouts, yes I suppose I must include Bob and Celia as having the availability of being able to sail out into the bay and then back without anyone seeing them.

Well that's everyone. Daniel is going to do a little digging along the harbour and at the boatyard."

"Well apart from the holiday cottages that is, I suppose." Said Alice.

"But they are only holiday-makers. Well except for the nerd, you know the computer guy, you'll have seen him in the Bay Hotel, skinny nerdy guy with glasses I believe he's taken to fishing although Andy MacFarlane said he's the most useless fisherman he's ever seen.

"So you and Daniel are becoming real friendly then, and don't tell me he just kissed you to further the investigation because I don't believe you, come on what was it like, he's a bit of alright isn't he, God when he gives you that thousand watts smile it makes your knees go to water. Does it do the same to you?"

"Alice Foster you are a married woman! But actually, you're right he has got the most gorgeous smile. And yes we did have a nice meal and a glass of wine and we chatted, which I enjoyed I must admit."

"And then he kissed you we saw it and so did most of the village."

"He kissed my cheek, that's all no great passion; I think he did it more out of devilment knowing you would all be watching than any great passion so don't get your knickers in a twist."

"But you're going up there tonight as I heard him ask you, so he must fancy you mustn't he?"

"You should have joined the police force Alice you would have been in plain clothes now, you would have made a first class interviewer thumb screws and all that. Yesss I'm going up to his place tonight but it will be to discuss what we have found out and toss a few ideas about… and yesss, we'll have a meal… and a drink… and alright I think he is very attractive."

This Sarah only said because Alice was indicating with her expression that Sarah was prevaricating and she was waiting for her to tell give in and tell her it was a date.

"I bet you can't look me in the eye Sarah Waters and tell me you don't fancy the pants off Daniel Summers…. Go on, go on I dare you, I'll be able to tell by your face if you lie to me."

"Ok, yes actually I do think he is rather gorgeous and I am enjoying his company, I think in some ways it reminds me of being in the force, not that I miss the force but I used to work with a lot of male colleagues and actually you miss their company. That is not to say that you fancied them all but … well you know what I mean about how different it is talking to a man than a woman… anyway the short answer is yes I fancy him .. There; are you happy now!?!"

"Ha, Hah I knew it; I knew you fancied the pants off him and ohh you lucky devil is all I can say."

Amazed that once Sarah had admitted to Alice her interest in Daniel was not purely work she seemed quite happy to go back to her café with the promise that mum was the word about any enquiries they were making.

Chapter 13

Sarah felt quite excited at the prospect of seeing Daniel again. It was a strange feeling, something she hadn't felt for a long time. The butterflies you got in your tummy during the day whenever you thought about your forthcoming meeting with a man, well someone you thought rather dishy.

As she walked the beach taking Scamp for his walk before she had a shower and changed into something feminine for a change she tried not to think too much about her visit to Daniel's, after all he could, in all seriousness, only be interested in the information she had gathered and to him the meeting was simply a meeting of minds.

It was such a beautiful night and the sun was still high, she thought she would wear her white wide leg linen trousers for coolness and her navy vest top with a large white anchor down the centre. The top was a stretchy material and showed off her slim figure and womanly curves to perfection. Putting her little stripy cotton pumps on her feet she surveyed her image in the mirror and was happy with the result, casual but smart she thought.

Sarah's tan was golden and her hair had become a beautiful streaked golden colour with the waves shining as she ran the comb through it for the second time in order to make sure she looked her very best.

She drove up the hill in her little jeep with a bottle of wine tucked into the glove box she took a deep breath in and breathing out slowly. Telling herself that she had dressed to please but even if it turned out that Daniel was only interested in the information she had dug up she wouldn't look too over dressed.

As she parked the car a wonderful smell drifted over towards her which tantalised her nostrils and she realised that Daniel was doing a BBQ, the table perched on the top of the hill had place settings and glasses all set out in readiness.

He must have heard the car because he came out of the house and Sarah's heart skipped that beat again, as he was dressed in navy cotton trouser shorts and a powder blue polo shirt, he had tanned muscular legs which suited shorts very well and on his feet he looked very much at home in his navy deck shoes.

Sarah blushed slightly as he caught her looking him up and down and wiggling his eyes brows he did the same without any shame at all at what he was doing.

"Mmm very nice, I must say," He said cheekily. This was just the type of thing Daniel would come out with, Sarah had began to notice.

"And you," Sarah shot back bravely eyeing him up and down in an imitation of what he had done to her.

"I hope you like BBQ? Madam?" He said while escorting Sarah over to the table to be seated. She gave him her bottle of wine although she said of course she couldn't drink much tonight as she was driving. The BBQ was excellent, and Sarah could see that Daniel was no novice as he had a huge gas BBQ and was pretty expert at cooking and serving.

The wine was refreshing and as they sat in companiable silence for a moment just enjoying the sound of the distant waves it was a shame to spoil it with any talk.

"Well I suppose I should tell you what I found out today with my ferreting? To be honest, not a lot."

Sarah decided not to mention Alice and Frank's little forgetful bookkeeping, though she did mention what Alice had heard about Bob, however Daniel already knew as the district nurse had already spoken to him just after Mary's death and Daniel had decided to use his own discretion and treat it as a mercy killing, telling the nurse to keep it to herself.

He had a good idea about Fat Charlie running bets and everyone knew that the Veach's at the post office were the centre for dodgy gossip but Daniel felt unlikely they were drug smugglers. That left the general dealers, which Daniel thought as everyone else did that they were highwaymen but not smugglers. This only left the Cockleshell Bay Hotel, and Bob and Celia.

"Oh and the computer nerd, you know the guy who's been in one of the holiday cottages for about six months Alice says he has taken up fishing recently."

"Well I mooched around the MacFarlane yard and they were quite clearly a bit nervous at what they thought I might find. But I didn't get the impression they were into anything as big as drug smuggling. They didn't appear to have money galore, and most of their stuff, Jet Ski's and dinghies looked possibly hooky but not terribly expensive, and it was mostly reconditioned no I can't see it being them this time.

"I asked them if they knew of anyone who went out fishing regularly or if they had seen anyone fishing who had never fished before and funnily enough they also said the nerdy guy, they said he seemed to fish with a fishing rod out in the deeper waters well that sounds a bit suspicious, I think he's worth a punt."

"So that means in the frame we have Bob and Celia who have the ability to get out to sea and back without anyone noticing, however there is no evidence that they seem to either have money troubles or excess money but they have to be suspects. Then there is the nerd, which seems little far fetched, have you seen him he looks as weak as a glass of water, he definitely looks like one of the computer geeks, but he also has to be a suspect."

"OK, now we must work out one month from the day the package was found and assume there could be another drop. We can use your telescope to see if there is any unusual lights out near the buoys at night, if that's OK with you?" Daniel said with a wiggle of his eyebrows, Sarah wondered how on earth he did that without looking like a sex pest but actually it just made him look incredibly naughty. And sexy.

"Did I hear you say you were in the Navy? Which was where you qualified as a diver? I bet you were a typical sailor with a woman in every port."

"I was not; I'll have you know that was one of the reasons why I left the Navy. It's actually a very lonely life and once I got to the rank of a lieutenant I decided enough was enough or I would never find a mate and get married, so I came out. The funny thing was I had always wanted to go to sea ever since I was a boy, you won't believe this but I was in the boy's brigade and the sea scouts, but of course I did my officer training at Dartmouth. Don't get me wrong I loved the Navy but I didn't want to make a career out of it instead of having a wife and family if you know what I mean?"

"So then you came out and joined the force, where did you end up working?"

"I was in Glasgow for two years when I finished my training, I was encouraged to take my sergeant's exam and passed, and it was then that I realised that the city wasn't for me. So I applied for a coastal posting, never thinking I would get one.

"By this time I was engaged, however my fiancée who was also in the force and thought she had hooked onto a rising star, had visions of big things for me in the future and was furious when she found out I had not only applied for, but was successful in getting the post of area sergeant at Cockleshell Bay, so she dumped me.

"So I left the Navy to find a wife, joined the police force and found a woman with good potential then threw it all away because I wanted to live by the sea, am I a fool or what?"

"No, I'm glad you followed you're heart to a place you obviously love and your style of policing suits the smaller villages, the friendly approach which has almost disappeared in the city. And if your fiancée had loved you she would have come with you, so she mustn't have been the right girl in my opinion."

"And what about you, have you ever been engaged? I know you haven't been married as I peaked into your records."

"Yes I was engaged once, however he had difficulty keeping his trousers on and on the final occasion it was with another police woman but it was in our bed. So I dumped him."

"Was the man a fool? Well he was certainly blind as he obviously could not see what he already had."

"Why thank you kind sir, and on that note I think I should be making a move. Thank you so much for a wonderful evening I've really enjoyed myself."

"Really? Does that mean you'll come again?"

"Really, and yes, I'll come again but don't forget you are more than welcome to come and share my telescope with me and we can gaze out to sea together."

Sarah knew that it was her, now being a little saucy, but their budding relationship seemed to be built on the kind of humour they both found a little risqué but quite innocent. As Sarah stood to walk towards her car Daniel took hold of one of her hands as they walked, and this gesture didn't seem in the least strange. When they reached the car before Sarah could climb inside Daniel moved closer and instead of a fleeting kiss on her cheek he placed his warm lips on hers and took all the time in the world but which was probably no more than a second to draw a response from Sarah's yielding and slightly parted lips.

He stood aside so that she could climb into the car and gave her the most outrageous wink with one of those gorgeous eyes, then he took a step back so that she could reverse and turn; she then drove slowly down the hill. When Sarah got back to her cottage it was very obvious she would never be able to sleep so she donned her thick cardigan and shouted for Scamp who was always ready for a walk and they went onto the deserted beach.

As she re-ran the nights events, what she'd said what he'd said and so on as you do when you want to relive something special when she began to hear that strange haunting music again. She stood for a moment saying to Scamp, "Listen, listen there it is that music, it's definitely 'Oh My Papa', I remember it well."

Before she realised that not only was she hearing music she was talking to her dog about it. Sarah laughed at her own old maid's behaviour, then as the music faded away into the shifting breeze as it always did she slowly walked back to her cottage and bed.

Chapter 14

The following morning just as Sarah was opening the shutters on the shop the phone rang, catching her off guard so she had to dash into the workshop to answer it. A little out of breath she answered, "Hi, Sarah's."

"You're out of breath; you're not dashing around are you?" Her mother's voice sounded concerned before telling Sarah she was calling to say she'd spoken to Bob at the Hotel and booked for the weekend arriving on the Friday which was tomorrow. Blanche said she hoped she hadn't made plans but it wouldn't matter anyway not wanting to spoil her plans and they would be more than happy to play dominoes and whist with Bob and Celia.

"No Mum that would be lovely, I'll see you then, is Dad OK?"

"Yes darling you know your Dad; happy as a sand boy, so we'll see you tomorrow night at the Bay."

Then she rang off, it suddenly dawned on Sarah that she would of course have to tell her parents about recent events, simply because she would feel uncomfortable about not being truthful with them. She decided to ring Daniel just to mention this although she was sure he would be fine with it. She found the number which he had given her of his private mobile rather than trying to catch him a the station office or his house where as he explained he spent very little time.

"Hi Daniel, its emm Sarah, I won't keep you if you're busy with a call or anything it's just a quickie."

"Hi Sarah, and slow down I'm not busy, I'm sat in a lay-by having a coffee so talk away, it's nice to hear from you by the way."

"Oh sorry, I sound rushed it's just–"

"I know you didn't want to bother me. Listen you couldn't bother me, not in that way take my word for it, now what can I do for you?"

"Well my parents are coming down for the weekend and…"

"You want me to disappear, you're embarrassed about me!!"

"No silly shut up and I'll tell you, no I really needed to know if I can take them into my confidence about the … current situation… just in case I say something and put my foot in it and I hate telling them fibs… you know?"

"Fibs wow I haven't heard that one spoken by a copper in a long time. Of course you must let them in on the actual parcel but keep our suspects out of the conversation OK? Where are they staying?"

"Well actually they stay at the Bay Hotel as I only have one bedroom and they hate my orthopaedic bed… Sorry you don't need to know that, I'm beginning to sound like my Mum…"

"Well yes you can mention the package but for goodness sake don't mention the fact that Bob and Celia are potential suspects… And by the way what's wrong with your bed?"

Sarah could just imagine his eyebrows dancing all over the place now that she had introduced beds into the conversation. Sarah decided on the spur of the moment to ask him to join her and her parents for a drink at the hotel if he was free.

"Well I'm on duty but I'm sure I could manage to pop in for a fruit juice. Thank you that would be very nice."

"Well I'll not keep you; I'll see you tomorrow night then any time after eight we'll be in the bar or the restaurant. Bye then."

Sarah was sure she had heard his laughter as she replaced the phone. The following evening when her Mum and Dad arrived they dropped their bags off and then came straight over to the shop. Ralph took Scamp onto the beach as he enjoyed the walk almost as much as Sarah did and missed the fresh air so much when he went home. Blanche sat on Sarah's sofa and suddenly said to Sarah.

"You look wonderful darling, and I don't just mean your lovely tan but you look really good…. I know what it is! You look happy… dare I say it you look even better than you did before you had the accident. Come on what is it? I know you love, this place and your little dog who is so sweet I know but there is something else!"

"Mum you are as bad as Alice, always trying to find me a date and fix me up, I'm perfectly capable of finding my own date when and if the time ever comes."

"Here's your father I'll ask him I bet he'll say you look different… I won't say a word… just see what he says."

"Did you enjoy your walk Dad, he's mad though isn't he?" Sarah said, nodding towards Scamp.

"Well I may as well tell you…"

"Aha, you didn't tell me but you'll tell your Father, I knew it, I knew it."

"Mum it's not what you think! A couple of weeks ago you know we had that absolutely terrible storm, do you remember me telling you about it? Well Scamp actually found a package that had washed up on the beach, he's a devil for finding stuff. Well the package it turns out was full of heroin! So of course there has been an investigation and all kinds going on, however there doesn't seem to be any way of knowing where it came from or who it belonged to… so that's what I was going to say…

"Mum thought like Alice there was a man involved," Sarah explained to her Dad, "and she swears blind I look different because I'm hiding something."

"Wow drugs, right here in Cockleshell Bay, no wonder you look bright as a button it must be a bit like being back in the force was it? Oh dear did it make you wish you were still in the force, we hoped you had forgotten about that part of your life."

"I know what you mean and I can see how you would think it might have upset me but do you know what I felt when Scamp found it? I was upset because I knew that my perfect idyllic life was going to be upset by the heavy footed coppers coming in to my village and I resented it, that's what I felt. Anway I passed it onto the local police sergeant and he has dealt with it all. Actually you'll meet him tonight I've asked him to call into the Bay for a drink with us. He won't be able to drink as he's on duty but he will call and say hello to you though."

Blanche and Ralph shared a look of 'I told you there was a man involved somewhere' when Sarah wasn't looking, then replied, "Oh, that'll be nice darling."

Blanche and Ralph went back to the hotel to dress for dinner giving Sarah a chance to have her walk on the beach before she also changed.

She took extra care to look nice even if she was only going to see Daniel for a few minutes she wanted to look, well, attractive, she supposed.

Blanche and Ralph were overjoyed at the prospect of meeting a friend of their daughter's. No matter how Sarah had tried to pass it off as matter of fact that this policeman was going to pop in, they knew their daughter looked happier than she had in over four years, longer actually if you counted the length of time she was with that no good fiancé of hers. They prayed that this chap was a different type even though he was yet another policeman.

When Sarah walked into the hotel's dining room both of her parents did a double take at how pretty she looked, and it wasn't simply that they were biased her being their daughter, but she looked stunning. It had been such a long time since they had actually seen her all dressed up as she was always in her uniform or casuals so this actually took their breath away.

Sarah had decided on a Batik print dress in shades of blue and aqua in a textured cotton and viscose. It had a flattering empire waist with short cap sleeves a deep rounded neckline, and the skirt flared out into an a –line design, the tie at the back meant you could pull in the waist for an ideal fit which in Sarah's case was very slim. With the dress she wore a pair of strappy sandals with a two-inch heel all of which gave her a look of sheer elegance.

Blanche was bursting with pride and knew without being hit over the head with a hammer that Sarah's appearance was all in aid of this 'Policeman who may call in for a drink'. She nudged her husband in the ribs and gave that 'I told you so' look that wives often do.

It was after their meal when Sarah and her parents were seated in the main bar area that Sarah spotted Bart and Andy Macfarlane all dressed in their Sunday best and leaning against the bar with pints in their hands and it appeared to be Bart that was flirting with the bar maid. Sarah could see why there was a slight snigger when people mentioned the very pretty girl's name which was Sally Fuller... it certainly didn't take brain of

Britain to see how the nickname had come about. She was the most endowed girl and unfortunately she was rather short in height which meant her heavy endowment tended to rest on the bar and give the punters rather a good view.

Andy on the other hand, was a little less forward although Sarah had heard that his interest lay elsewhere with Josie Small, the trainee manageress from the post office. However Sarah had also heard from Alice that he had not been able to pluck up the courage to ask her out, so the only time he could speak to her was if he went into the post office on the pretext of taxing his vehicle's or to ask for stamps.

Just as Ralph stood up to go to the bar to buy drinks the door opened and in walked Daniel, looking devilishly handsome in his uniform, cap in hand he glanced around the room and saw instantly where Sarah was sitting. He, like Ralph and Blanche before him, took a double take at how lovely she looked this evening, and as he entered Sarah stood up to greet him, affording him a perfect look at her stunning image and her welcoming smile was all Blanche needed to confirm that there was something very special about this chap.

As Daniel came over to the group he held out his hand to Blanche giving her that thousand watt smile and the wink of the eye saying he could see where Sarah had got her looks from, making Blanche go weak at the knees. He then turned his attention to Ralph, saying how nice it was to meet him and addressed him as 'sir',which was the icing on the cake. From then on they were both putty in his hands although he had managed it in all innocence that was the strange thing about Daniel Summers, he was actually a natural charmer.

Daniel insisted on buying the drinks and wouldn't hear of Ralph buying anything.

"I'm on orange juice I'm afraid, as I'm on duty tonight however tomorrow night is my night off and I would love to take you all out to dinner."

"No, no we wouldn't dream of it, you must be our guest tomorrow night here, the meals are wonderful and we would look forward to that very much, any friend of Sarah's is certainly a friend of ours."

"Well thank you that would be lovely I would love to do that, and I'm certainly doing my best to become a friend of your daughter, however she's very choosy who she takes as a friend but I'm working on it."

He flashed his gorgeous smile again before excusing himself, until tomorrow night then and it's been a pleasure to meet you both. He said goodnight to Sarah and actually took hold of her hand for a split second before wandering over to the bar to say a cheerful good evening to Andy and Bart before leaving the hotel.

"Wow." said Blanche and Sarah laughed out loud.
"Mother, at your age, although I forgive you he is a charmer isn't he?"

"A charmer, and he is lovely he was at the front of the queue when they gave out the good looks wasn't he and he also has the charm to go with it."

Then Ralph contributed with a man's point of view, saying normally he can suss out a fraud or a 'wideboy', but he just seemed genuine, a really nice lad.

"He is, and I know what you mean though, the first time I met him I was a bit sledgehammer Mum, you think it can't be true but actually it is. He is actually as nice a person on the inside as he is on the outside if that's possible. Ha, Ha, and Dad you don't have to worry he certainly isn't a 'wideboy' he's honest and open, believe me."

Chapter 15

The following morning Ralph sat in the shop so that Sarah and Blanche could go shopping and have a couple of hours together doing girly things. On the way back they had a bite to eat at the café, Sarah was glad she had clued her Mum in on the parcel before Alice spilled the beans. Luckily Alice wasn't aware of Sarah and Daniel's suspects or she would have been telling Blanche about that too.

They closed the shop early that afternoon and all three went for a walk along by the harbour taking Scamp with them to chase the huge seagulls which were almost as large as him, before slowly walking back. Sarah thought how nice it was to have her parents fit and well enough to be able to travel down to visit her, and how lucky all three of them were that this was not four years ago when life had become a nightmare. It seemed at the time as though there was no light at the end of the tunnel, yet here they were strolling along looking out to the most beautiful sea view with a wonderful beach and soft sea breezes, what more could a person want.

Blanche and Ralph went back to the hotel to have a little rest before the evening meal which had been arranged for seven thirty to eight. This gave Sarah a chance for her usual walk on the beach with Scamp then a long bath and hair wash before deciding what she would wear. Although she made light of it not being a date to her parents, Sarah's preparations were very much of the date nature. She hung various outfits on the front of the wardrobe doors and then reduced them by preference until the number was reduced to the one she would finally wear, if that wasn't preparing for a date she didn't know what was! However she still denied that she was thinking of it as a date just a meal with her parents and a guest, Who just happened to be Daniel.

Sarah had narrowed it down and her eventual choice was to look cool but casual, not overdressed as he had already seen her in a smart dress, but not too casual as he had also seen her in her beach clothes. No she must look chic, but casual, so her final choice was a top of pure linen, tunic style in eggshell with a stand collar, three quarter length sleeves with vents in the cuffs; it was long line and also had vents up the sides. Over the tunic she wore a waistcoat which was very Chinese in style with the knot button fastenings in a tiny black herringbone; teamed with those, she wore a pair of linen weave cropped trousers which also gave the Chinese look, and a pair of flat post and toe sandals.

Giving herself the final once over in the mirror she left for the Hotel. As she walked into the dining room Daniel was already seated with her parents. A good sign, thought Sarah as it meant all three were early which went down extremely well with her parents as they hated to be kept waiting. It was one of those little things that had irritated them about her ex-fiancé, another was that he always smelled of drink which meant he had had time to go for a drink yet he couldn't be on time to meet his future in-laws.

"Hi everyone, I hope I haven't kept you waiting even though I came five minutes early."

As Daniel stood up to greet her and pull out her chair Sarah got a full view of him all dressed up in his Sunday best, and 'wow!' was all she could think, Colin Firth couldn't have looked more handsome in his pure wool navy blazer and underneath he wore a JT [Joseph Tuner] candy striped shirt open at the neck showing his tanned face and neck off to perfection and wonderful cream chinos and of course you could have seen your face in the shine on his loafers. If that hadn't surprised her enough for one night, his next move almost blew her away.

As he pulled her chair out for her to sit he casually gave her a kiss on her cheek… there and then.. in front of her parents… who instead of being shocked were quite obviously delighted.

"You were definitely worth waiting for and you're right you aren't late we all got here a little early, as it's a habit of mine I'm afraid I actually hate being late, and I know it irritates some people that I always arrive first, but it's habit."

Ka- ching thought Sarah, second point to Daniel, and if this carried on her parents would be booking the church before they left to go home. The meal was a great success, her parents were quite obviously taken with Daniel and who wouldn't be.? He was witty, good looking, entertaining. He had a responsible job and they could see by the look on Sarah's face that she really liked him. They could also see that Daniel was very attracted to Sarah and after everything she had been through their fervent hope was that Daniel was the one!!

Daniel had ordered a brandy for Ralph as he said he enjoyed a brandy before going off to bed however Blanche stood up and excused herself yawning, explaining that the fresh air usually did this to her when she came down to see Sarah. Daniel thanked them both for a wonderful meal and offered to escort Sarah across to her flat, which she accepted, sure that her parent's excuses were in order that Daniel could say good night to Sarah without any embarrassment.

Daniel took Sarah's hand in his as they walked out into the evening, the sky was full of stars but it was still warm. As they got to the door of the flat Sarah opened the door and out like a flying bullet flew Scamp and straight onto the beach, so as casually as they had walked across the road they walked hand in hand along the firm sand where the tide had gone out.

"Thank you Sarah I've had a wonderful evening. Your parents are lovely, I can see where you got your personality from. You have your mother's looks and your father's determination."

"Listen, can you hear anything?" Sarah said as they walked along the beach. "Do you know that sometimes when I walk here on the beach alone at night, when the wind is in a certain direction, you'll think I'm mad but I actually hear…music."

Daniel suddenly made a coughing noise in the dark and Sarah took it that he was actually scoffing her and she carried on in an attempt to convince him.

"No… I mean only sometimes, I mean I don't hear it all the time you know, just sometimes when the wind is right."

"Ermm.. and what kind of music is it you hear; I mean is it Jazz or guitar or what,?"

"No…. and don't scoff, I really hear it, and it's actually, well.. the trumpet actually! I know you're laughing at me, but I swear I'm not mad, I can even tell you the tune because my Dad used to have a record which he used to play at full blast every Sunday morning when I was a teenager and they called it Eddie Calvert's golden trumpet, or some such thing and the tune I hear all the time is 'Oh My Papa', I even asked Dad if he had heard it when he took Scamp out on the beach but he hadn't but he does remember the tune very well."

Sarah pushed him playfully in the ribs saying he thought she was mad didn't he Daniel slipped his arm around her shoulders, saying if that's what she heard then he believed every word of it. His arm felt warm and comforting and she could have stayed like that for hours, just walking and talking, with the gentle sound of the waves lapping on the shore.

They gradually turned around and began their slow walk back and as they arrived at her door Daniel led her inside, pulling back slightly so that he could see her face, his own face descended slowly until his lips touched hers and he felt her intake of breath and the catch in her throat as she gave a slight gasp. Sarah was sure she could feel his heart pounding through his shirt as she rested her hands on his chest. Then all too soon it was over and Daniel stepped back touching her fingers momentarily before slowly walking away with that devilish wink of the eye.

Chapter 16

Early on the Sunday morning Ralph wandered over to the beach as he could see Sarah and Scamp doing their usual ritual of beach combing, the fact that it was Sunday made absolutely no difference to Sarah, interesting stuff was still interesting even on a Sunday. A wave from Ralph signalled Scamp to launch himself up the beach to greet his visitor.

"Morning Darling, what a beautiful day, it's always a pity to go when the weather is so lovely."

"Then don't go there's nothing stopping you staying on is there?"

"Well, we have other things on you know, your mother's involved in WI things and I have a golf date tomorrow, you know, busy busy. Listen Sarah, a strange thing happened last night which I thought I better tell you about."

"Well you know I had a brandy before going up to bed and you know I shouldn't, but I enjoy one, so I did, please don't tell me off as your mother has already beaten you to it. Well after going to bed I began to get the most awful heartburn so in the end I had to go down to the kitchen and get a glass of ice water and some anti acid tablets. Which was when I heard some voices. Well I moved to follow where they were coming from and eventually stopped outside the snug door, and as I pushed the door open a crack I nearly died of fright. There must have been a dozen pairs of eyes silently staring at me all sat at tables and holding playing cards in their hands.

"Well it was obvious I had stumbled in on something and it was then that Bob appeared out of nowhere with a tray of drinks in his hand and suggested he explained what was happening. So there I was sat in the snug in the middle of the night in my dressing gown drinking tonic water. When Bob explained that this was the weekly card school, although it is normally held on a Friday night. But would you believe it, who should walk into the bar last night but Daniel all dressed in his uniform and they thought he must have been tipped off, so they postponed the game until tonight. Well I had to laugh because when I explained to them that Daniel had simply come in while on duty at your invitation and even then he only had an orange juice before going, there was no official visit. And then of course last night when he arrived again but they soon decided that if he was on a date with a girl as pretty as you, he wouldn't be interested in coming back to the pub to check up on a lock in, now would he?

"But the funniest thing is Sarah it had crossed my mind and I'm so glad that I was wrong because I like Bob and Celia very much and so does your Mum, but you know that old grate that's on the beach? You know the one it looks like the entrance to the pub, I bet it goes right underneath and in to the cellars, well it crossed my mind that maybe Bob and Celia were involved in that drugs thing you know, after all who would know if they rowed out to sea and collected parcels of drugs?"

"Oh Dad you're priceless and also it must certainly be you I take after, Bob and Celia were on our list of suspects but Daniel and I agreed not to mention it to you and Mum because we knew you liked them very much and we didn't want to upset you or implicate you. Daniel said I took after my father and he is so right, as we both have a suspicious nature yet we both want to think the best of people. So in the end all it is, is that they have an illegal lock-in where they play cards?"

"Yes but you won't do anything about it will you? They won't get into to trouble will they? I'd hate that and it's not doing anyone any harm now is it?"

"Don't worry, you can even tip Bob the wink before you go and tell him not to panic, Daniel isn't interested in small things like that. He's a really nice guy and you can tell Bob to carry on as normal Daniel will not be checking up on Fridays or Saturday nights at the Bay Hotel."

Blanche and Ralph left with a wave and a smile, happier than when they normally left Sarah behind. It wasn't that they thought on previous occasions that she was unhappy because they knew she wasn't. They also knew she had made the right choice, but they did wonder how on earth she was ever going to find anyone. Someone who could give her the male company, which a woman of her age should have before burying herself away in a tiny village and becoming a mad old beachcomber for the rest of her life no matter how idyllic the village.

Sarah thought she had better let Daniel know what her Dad had found out and so called his mobile, however it went straight to voice mail so she left a brief message and said she would speak to him later. After going for her walk along the beach and then having her usual treat with Alice, who wanted to know every detail about her night out with her parents and Daniel. Pretty much a blow by blow account, telling Sarah she had seen them come out of the Bay all dressed up and walk towards the beach where she had lost sight of them as it was dark so she wanted Sarah to fill in the bits she missed.

"Alice you are ridiculous, have you stopped watching your television all together now that I have moved here? It must play havoc with your home life having to spend so much time at the window watching little old me."

"Listen, your potential sex life is my television, you and Daniel are better than any soap on telly. There is certainly nobody better looking than him in any of the soaps. God he looked gorgeous in his smart clothes on Saturday night, did he impress your parents? Did your Mum just swoon at the sight of those eyes and that killer wink he does?"

"Ha, actually you're spot on, he did knock my Mum's socks off with his killer smile and yes the wink just made her hot flush creep up her neck until she was almost gasping for air. The thing is Dad liked him, which means a lot to me as my Dad is a good judge of character. He was right about my rogue fiancé I knew that yet he never let on in case it hurt me.

"But what the hell, Daniel is a friend that's all, the poor guy has no idea how many people are trying to marry him off, if I was him I'd run for the hills before it's too late."

"Go on you'd miss him something awful if he wasn't here I bettya."

"Well… Actually Alice you're right, he has brought a certain excitement into my life."

"You mean he has brought an 'oomph' to your life, a red blooded woman needs sex and he has that in spades."

"My God Alice you really call a spade a spade don't you? Ha, ha, ha."

Sarah left Alice's in a good fettle, which she always did. Alice was a tonic and a good friend, Sarah knew she had been the luckiest person alive when she moved to Cockleshell Bay, although she may have had her doubts in the beginning she certainly hadn't ever looked back.

Sarah could see there was a message on her phone and it was from Daniel, and was sorry she had missed the opportunity to speak to him; however she was more than happy after hearing his message. He wanted to know if she was allowed to close the shop tomorrow and go on a picnic. They were to take his launch and nip to one or two of the small coves, and Scamp was very welcome to come too. Could she let him know so that he could prepare the picnic. Texting him back in

case he was busy at work she said she
and Scamp would love to come on his
picnic and as she was the boss then she
was allowed to close the shop whenever
she wanted.

Chapter 17

The arrangement was that he would collect Sarah and Scamp at nine o'clock in the morning; assuring her he had checked the weather, which he was sure would be perfect for them.

One look at the weather told Sarah it was definitely going to be a hot one so she wore her pale lemon bathing costume under a pair of khaki shorts and a lemon linen blouse and the obligatory flip flops so handy when you were constantly in water.

Daniel arrived before time as usual so it was a good job she had been ready with a bag packed for at least fifteen minutes. She knew enough about the weather to take a cardigan or a jacket in case of a sea fret. Daniel's dinghy was moored at the harbour; it was a hard bodied launch which looked about twelve feet long with a metal frame across the top on which he had fixed the spot lights so important for night work. It didn't take Daniel very long to uncover the boat and stabilise the outboard. Then they were off.

It was very comfortable with two seats not unlike car seats, Sarah held onto Scamp's collar for a while until he realised that if he didn't sit still he would be in the drink. Sarah knew that Scamp was no fool and before long he sat comfortably just letting the wind blow in his face and making no attempt to go anywhere.

"I want to show you something but I want it to look to anyone who may be looking through binoculars that we are just out for a day in the sunshine."

"I see, so you do suspect that whoever it is has a sea view and is watching all the time?"

"Without a doubt, I actually think we both know who the pick- up man is but he isn't the big fish, but I'm sure he could lead us to him and it's Mr Big that we need to concentrate on."

As the boat twisted and turned to anyone watching it was as though Daniel and Sarah were simply out for a little run in his boat. They neared the buoy with the red rope that Daniel had mentioned when he had inspected all the buoys.

"Now as we pass the buoy try and look back and see if you can spot your house from here, I want to know if you would be able to see with your telescope any activity in this location, you won't have to know the exact spot because it would be at night that you would be watching so there would be lights."

"Yes, I'm sure there would be a clear view, yes I can actually see without making a big thing and getting out the binoculars I'm sure that's my flat window."

"Good, I thought so and now we are going to look as though we haven't been looking at this spot and sort of slalom for a few miles until we're out of site of the village, are you ready hang on tight?"

They came to rest at a tiny little beach which appeared to be deserted and which mirrored her little beach, apart from the fact it was smaller and further up the coast. Daniel expertly dropped the anchor and the water was shallow enough to wade into the shore carrying the picnic and blanket.

"This is beautiful Daniel, I've lived here all this time and never been here before, to be honest I'm so content with my own little beach I never think to explore further up the coast."

Once they had arranged the blanket Sarah was eager to know if Daniel thought the same as her that the pick up guy had to be the nerd.
"What makes you so sure though, Daniel?"

"Well to be honest, I've been driving Bart and Andy Macfarlane mad; I have rather deliberately been very, very, visible at their boat yard, so much so that cars have even done a u-turn when they've seen the squad car. I have deliberately made sure they have noticed my presence and so has any visitors or business associates that may have wanted to do any business. If you get my meaning, they then drive off in a cloud of dust, leaving a very angry Bart Macfarlane."

"Actually I saw you say hello to the brothers on Friday evening, little did you realise that you frightened half of the village that night and not just the Macfarlane brothers."

"Well I did that on purpose so that they would feel I had eyes everywhere so when I offered them a solution to their problem i.e. me, they would be responsive enough to agree."

"And what was your proposition then, to the brothers?"

"I simply said that every time they saw the nerd go out fishing no matter what time of day or night they had to call me on my mobile. But if they didn't and I found out, then I would begin to reappear at their yard, I said I may even decide to take my coffee breaks outside in their forecourt. It was amazing how helpful they were after that."

"Ha, ha, you are a clever devil aren't you? And obviously you have some sort of proof about the nerd then?"

"Oh yes, the brothers have seen him go out in his boat and appear to be fishing, as though it were a regular practice, however he has never brought any fish back not even once, and the line doesn't even appear to be baited and he carries no equipment, no it's simply a cover so that when he does go out to collect the parcel and then pass it on to someone else no one would suspect him. Also while he was out 'fishing' I went to have a look at his holiday cottage, and as he's supposed to be such a computer nerd I wondered why he simply had a laptop and it looked to be a fairly old one at that. No I think he is simply the point of contact I think he collects the package and then he delivers it somewhere else. "

"Well I think we can rule Bob and Celia out now. Poor Dad he was so worried, he's taken a real liking to them and thought he had stumbled upon some sort of smugglers den that turned out to be an illegal lock-in, and a card school. They must have almost died of fright when you arrived in the hotel on Friday night in your uniform. So Bob came clean and told Dad all about it, they had put the card school off on the Friday night thinking they had been rumbled by you, when all the time it was Bart and Andy you were after and they must have thought you had radar knowing they would be in the Bay on a Friday night.

Listen, I half promised Dad that you would turn a blind eye to Bob's card school and lock-in. I hope I wasn't talking out of turn after all you are the bobby in Cockleshell Bay."

"Don't worry I'm not interested in lock-ins or card schools, and to be honest it helps in the long run as you know, if you give out one or two favours then they are more likely to help in the future with some other little misdemeanour, if you ask them."

Sarah was relieved for her Dad and Bob's sake.

Daniel began to dig in the sand until he had made two very comfortable sand seats and a table to have their picnic. They laid the blanket properly over the seated area and unpacked the picnic, Then Daniel unpacked a bottle of wine and two glasses much to Sarah's delight.

"This is going to be a lot different to the picnics I usually go to, mine usually consist of egg sandwiches and orange juice, your picnic is a much better idea."

The sun was very warm and they decided in a moment of madness to swim before they ate or drank in case as Sarah said sensibly, "one of them got cramp". Sarah said her mother would never let her go swimming after she had eaten for at least an hour, to which Sarah's imagination told her she would have sank like a stone.

Having not actually taken as many clothes off in front of anyone since she had been in hospital Sarah was a little shy, however knowing she had her swimsuit on underneath meant she simply had to take off her shorts and blouse and run for the sea without looking back and seeing the expression on Daniel's face.

She knew without looking his eyebrows would have wiggled and immediately made her blush without saying a word. There were no outward scars to Sarah's injuries, except on her spine and they were largely unobtrusive. She had a good figure she knew that, but her relationship with her fiancé and his relentless search for something better made her feel as though she lacked in some way as a woman.

Daniel raced after her diving in the cool water with a splash. They both surfaced at the same time, laughing at the coolness of the water.

"It's chilly, you can hardly believe how cold it is when it's so hot on the beach, it tempts you to jump in then freezes you."

They splashed about for a while laughing like children on a hot summer's day, before deciding enough was enough. As they came out of the sea, shaking the excess water from their bodies, Sarah guessed without turning around that Daniel was taking an appreciative look at her shapely form as she walked up the beach. But for some reason she had suddenly found her confidence, and turning to see if she was right her gaze fell on his beautiful figure, lean, dark and very, very handsome, and it was her who was caught looking.

They lay in the sun and dried out sipping their wine and eating Daniel's professionally made picnic. It was then that Sarah decided this was the place to explain about her past and why she had ended up in Cockleshell Bay.

"This is the first time I've had a swimsuit on since before my accident, not that I swam a lot before but at least my back hadn't been broken and then put back together again. You know when you are bed ridden for any length of time you quickly turn to jelly."

"Well that certainly has not happened to you, if I may say so you have a fabulous figure."

"Why thank you, although I wasn't fishing for compliments."

They lay on their makeshift seats which Daniel had deliberately sculpted close to each other so that when you lay down you couldn't fail to touch. The sun on their faces and their eyes closed Sarah began to tell Daniel about her life before she came to Cockleshell Bay.

She explained how she had loved the force and had only been driving with Stevie Thomson for a few weeks, he had been transferred into Glasgow from somewhere in the North and her now ex-partner had taken his sergeant's exam and moved on to another area.

"Sarah you don't have to tell me unless you want too, I know you well enough now to know that you were not in anyway to blame."

"No I want to tell you and then it will be said and forgotten. You know about the car chase and the young lad Terry, well he was a habitual joyrider although why they call it that I'll never know because there is no joy involved. Anyway Terry wasn't bad he was just a bit of a pain and a total waste of police time. And it was swings and roundabouts sometimes you caught these jokers and other times you didn't, it's all just part of the job, you have to learn to bide your time and not loose your cool.

"Stevie couldn't do that, we had Terry cornered there was no way out for him, and if Stevie had left him alone Terry would have jumped out of the car and legged it. But Stevie couldn't have that… he deliberately drove the squad car at Terry in his Ford Fiesta. I saw his face, I'll never forget the terrified expression on his face, and then it all happened in slow motion until I woke up in hospital.

"My spine was broken in two places and the prognosis was that I would spend the rest of my life in a wheelchair. I lost my job, my career, my flat and my independence and if something inside me hadn't told me to fight on, be strong fight back, don't give in that's where I would be, in a wheelchair.

"My parents were a tower of strength, they gave me the courage, they put up with my moods and my anger and they never ever questioned my motives they just supported me. My Dad drove me to physiotherapy, day after day after day and sat and waited until I had punished myself enough and was mentally and physically exhausted, he never judged, never tried to dissuade me from going, he was just there for me.

"And through it all you know what hurt me the most? It was not the pain from my injuries, but the disappointment in those people, those so-called friends and colleagues, people I had worked with and put my life on the line for. Oh in the beginning there are the flowers and the cards and the get well soon's. But that soon dies away and so does their interest in you as a person.
"But during all of my rehabilitation I knew that my turn would come to speak out at the hearing, that kept me going, and I intended to shock everyone by walking into the court and telling the truth, not the version that Stevie Thomson had told me to say. The one

and only time he came to visit me, he said that if I didn't tell them that the accident was Terry's fault and unavoidable he would make life very difficult for me. The look he gave me that day when I was sat in my wheelchair was pure evil, I'll never forget his grin as though it wasn't his fault it was everyone else's fault and I would have to back his story or be sorry he would make sure of it.

"Well that only made me more determined that I would nail his hide to the wall if it killed me. However on the day of the hearing I was far from strong enough to stand for the whole length of the court proceedings so I had to use my wheelchair. The evidence that Stevie had presented, plus Terry's prior charges coupled with the seriousness of my injuries the judge ruled that due to the severity of my injuries my judgement was clouded and therefore my testimony was unreliable.

"As we left the courtroom it struck me that no one except the old duty sergeant had taken the time to come to the hearing. And even though I knew that after a few more weeks I would be stronger and able to walk, and probably be able to return to the force in some capacity or other, even a desk job. It was the realisation that I could never go back and I certainly could never sit at a desk but most of all I could never go and work with those people who called themselves my friends yet didn't believe in me enough to come and listen to my version of the accident that made my mind up to leave and make a fresh start somewhere else.

"I have never looked back from the day I came to Cockleshell Bay on a little holiday to please my parents, I've loved it and have never looked back and I never will."

Sarah sat up and looking down into Daniel's dark eyes as he sat propped up and leaning on his elbow, he had been looking down on Sarah as she had told her story. He hadn't spoken as he knew that Sarah had bottled this up for a long time and the fact that she had chosen to tell him was a sign that she trusted him and he hoped, liked him enough to let him in on her deep feelings of sadness and hurt at not only her profession but those she had called friends.

Daniel reached out and took hold of Sarah's hand saying to her as he looked into her eyes, "We are so lucky, you and I."

"And how do you make that out Sergeant Summers?"

"We were both given a second chance, and we both had the courage to take it and here we are, and I know where I would rather be and with whom at this present moment don't you?"

Sarah thought for a split second.

"Do you know something, you're right… you are so bloody right, I haven't been so happy since… well actually I can't remember…"

It was then that Daniel pulled her gently by the hand he had been holding on top of him.

"And I haven't been so happy since you arrived at my station with the dreaded and very much unwanted package. Although I must say it's been great fun working with my beautiful new assistant, it makes a change from sweaty old coppers from Glasgow."

Daniel's lips tasted of salt and as his hands slid up and down her spine rhythmically Sarah could feel her bones melting. Her hand automatically found their way into his lush thick black hair as she kissed him as thoroughly as he kissed her and as his gentle probing thumbs slid up and down the material of her swimsuit she could feel her nipples harden beneath his touch.

Daniel knew that they should stop now although the cove was idyllic it was still a public place and he could think of more private and comfortable places to make love to a beautiful woman, and someone he had come to care for very much.

Taking a deep breath and pulling Sarah up by the hand, he began a slow walk along the shore, still holding her hand and rhythmically rubbing his thumb back and forth in her palm. Sarah knew he was using an awful lot of restraint and she had sympathy with him as she also felt as though she could quite easily have done a Debra Carr and Burt Lancaster in the surf, but slow and steady wins the day, her Mum used to say when she became over excited about something Sarah really wanted, the right time will present itself.

They had had a perfect day and as the sun cooled they packed away their picnic and began the short boat ride home. As they carried their picnic basket and blanket back to the car to any onlookers it would look as though they had simply been out for the day and hopefully not aroused any suspicion.

Daniel dropped Sarah at her flat and made arrangements to come the following evening to watch for any lights or unusual activity in that area.

"My turn to cook, and thank you Daniel."

"For what?"

"For a lovely day out, I've really enjoyed our picnic together."

It was quite clear to Daniel exactly what she meant and he gave her the most outrageously sexy wink.

"God, your expressions should be censored do you know that?"

"It's not the looking you have to worry about it's the touching." He said again with the wiggle of the eyebrows and then he was gone, away up the hill.

Chapter 18

The next few nights were taken up taking turns watching through Sarah's telescope, looking for unidentified lights near the buoy. Their evenings were spent pleasantly sharing stories about their past lives.

Daniel talked about the Navy and how at one time he really thought his future lay there until he said jokingly, "Mother Nature tugged my string and reminded me that a man needs a mate."

Yet again he had that suggestive look which Sarah had become familiar and comfortable with. Sarah's history was similar in a way she had thought her career lay in the police force until she too would marry and have a family; however it wasn't to be for either of them. Or had Mother Nature something better in store for both of them?

It was on Friday afternoon just before closing time that Daniel parked the police car in the Bay car park as he had over the last few nights. Expecting a late finish as usual and not wanting it to look as though he was staying overnight at Sarah's flat giving rise to village gossip, Sarah said for him to nip up and make the coffee while she locked up.

Just as she was switching off the display cabinet lights and about to lock the front door the bell dinged signalling a last minute customer. Sarah muttered something about having all day then arriving at closing time but looked up with her ready smile on her face. However that smile was to freeze in place as the last person she ever expected to see was standing in her shop in front of her.

"Well, well, well, Sarah Waters, Miss Ironsides herself, so you're the Sarah of Sarah's jewellery, I might have known it. You just couldn't keep your nose out of police business could you? When they said who had handed in the parcel to the local PC Plod I never guessed."

"Sarah's throat had gone dry and her heart was pounding but she recovered enough to ask what he was doing here this couldn't be his district as this area was policed by Sergeant Daniel Summers."

"Ah yes, the local wooden top, I work for Her Majesty's Customs and Excise and I'm in charge of this case. This is too big for the local bobby."

It was then that something made Stevie look up to the open door which led to

Sarah's flat, and standing on the stair looking completely at home was Daniel looking just a little bit gorgeous in his black short sleeved uniform with muscles that could have crushed Stevie's smarmy face in a second.

"Introduce me, Sarah" Said Daniel in a menacing tone that meant he had overheard Stevie's insults to both him and her.

"Daniel, this is Stevie Thomson, my ex co-driver and who apparently is now working for the Customs and Excise, Stevie this is Daniel Summers, area Sergeant of this county."

"Ah so that's the way the land lies, shacking up with the local bobby, next best thing to actually doing the job, eh Sarah?"

Sarah moved to say something but Daniel who had came down the stairs silently and was beside her by this time touched her arm and moved menacingly to stand directly in front of Stevie and towering over him by a good three inches in height and much more in sheer masculine bulk.

"I'll say this only once Mr Thomson. Firstly you are an APO which is an assistant preventative officer with the HMCE, and you certainly do not outrank me in this investigation. But if you come through that door again and speak to Sarah in that manner, you will go out through that window, is that clear?"

Stevie's sickly grin slipped a bit as he took a step back saying who was going to do that, when Daniel placed one hand on his shoulder and gripped, whatever it was that he did it was enough to take the grin completely off Stevie's face and his colour changed from pink to very, very pale.

"Hey, hey just joking mate, no probs, if that's the way the wind blows, good on ya." Stevie muttered as he made for the door, but Sarah stopped him before he left knowing she would probably never see him again, she just had to ask.

"So why the change of 'career' as I remember your budding career was more important to you than telling the truth in court."

" Ah well not that it means anything now but I wasn't going to stay where I wasn't wanted, bunch of w– that old Sergeant had it in for me and spread rumours, that's all they were, but of course they loved their poor little Sarah who ended up in a wheelchair."

As he left the shop slamming the door behind him the air seemed to be sucked out of Sarah's body. Locking the door and leaning against it as though she was locking out the big bad wolf. Daniel took hold of her gently and just held her tight for a moment, before leading her up the stairs to the flat.

"How did you know that he was only an assistant whatever his title was, you brought him down a peg or two and really took the wind out of the pompous twits sails didn't you?"

"Ah my darling, you've been out of the job too long, have you forgot I can do anything with the press of a button on my trusty little computer phone. I knew he had just joined and knew he could only have been an assistant as he hadn't had time to be anything else and I obviously hit the spot as he didn't deny it now did he? Anyway, are you alright?"

"Yes … but am I glad you were here. Do you see what he's like its not the kind of threat you can fight, he has a way of putting things that makes you feel as though his is the only word and no one would believe what you said."

"But, I get the feeling that you always had an ally at the station and he made life very difficult for Mr Thomson so difficult I have a feeling that his only route was out."

"You know I think you're right, he did come to the hearing, my old sergeant and he did wish me well as I was leaving with my parents although I was so upset at the outcome, I probably didn't have very much to say to him. But it's nice to know I wasn't forgotten."

Daniel's arms which had been wrapped loosely around Sarah gave a little squeeze before he lifted a hand putting one finger under her chin and lifted her face so that he could gaze into her eyes, saying.

"Anyone who ever met you, Sarah Waters could never forget you."

And with those words his lips descended on her soft mouth. Their kisses seemed to be driven, his was born from a feeling of wanting to protect the person he had come to care for very much, and hers was from a need to feel loved at that moment from someone she felt closer to than anyone ever before.

The outcome was inevitable as their passion arose and they each began to strip off the others clothing all the while making their way towards to Sarah's bedroom. They both knew that this was what they had wanted each time they had said a tortured goodnight and now it was almost as though they couldn't wait or bear the feelings of pure joy they brought to each other.

Their passion eventually satiated not unlike the calm that came after a storm when the waves lapped gently on the shore. Daniel played with Sarah's hair as she lay on his chest with her eyes closed, but with a permanent smile on her face, knowing she could touch or feel this gorgeous body now without feeling in the least embarrassed she gave out a little giggle.

"What? What's tickling your fancy?"

Again Sarah knew exactly the look he would have on his face as he said those suggestive words.

"You are, do you know how many times I wanted to actually touch you… you know you're a devilishly handsome man even my Mum fancied you but I was the one that got you."

"God you make me feel like a prize, I'll have you know there are lots of women out there who are totally turned off by me and my lifestyle. Well they must, because I tried hard enough to get a date and didn't have a great deal of success and even my fiancée dumped me when I wouldn't 'rise to the occasion' so to speak."

Sarah giggled at the very obvious double meaning which he knew only too well exactly what he was saying.

"And if it comes to prizes you are the prize, Glasgow's finest's loss is my gain. And although I would never ever want you to be hurt again, if you hadn't you would never have come to Cockleshell Bay and I would never have found you. When I look at you I see a very beautiful and intelligent woman, when girls look at me they think I'm an empty headed if rather good looking [said tongue in cheek] wooden top as your ex-partner described me."

"You really don't know your women then, the minute I saw you…."

"Yes… you didn't see my brain now did you? Be honest?" Daniel was saying playfully remembering only too well what he was wearing the first time they met.

"I… did… I did… it was just hidden underneath... Erm your boxer shorts… no I'm kidding, I'm kidding." Sarah said as Daniel began to tickle her.

"How can I put this without sounding arrogant. Imagine how a platinum blonde actress feels when the only parts she is ever offered are those of a dumb blonde, she could be a scientist with a string of qualifications to her name yet no one sees her as anything but a dumb blonde. Do you see what I mean?"

"I do see what you mean, but Daniel you had a wonderful career in the Navy and you could have a sparkling career in front of you if you wanted, but you have chosen to enjoy your life in a place you love and you certainly don't have to worry about what others think of you, do you? And being gorgeous looking doesn't have to be a drawback." Daniel pulled her closer indicating that he understood what she was saying and was grateful to her.

"Hey… you OK? Daniel said giving Sarah a comforting squeeze… "After your visit from your ex?"

"Yeah... I was just a bit taken back, I mean I never expected in a million years to see his slimy twofaced grin again, especially in my little shop. But yes as long as I have my new partner to fight the good fight, and we can search out criminal activity like Batman and Robin I'm good, in fact I'm more than good."

"Hey…" Said Daniel back with that suggestive tone which Sarah knew heralded some outrageous comment.

"I don't care what your parents think about this bed… I love it, as long as you're in it with me."

Stevie Thomson was soon forgotten as they rolled together laughing with pure joy and the pleasure of each other.

Chapter 19

It was the following night before Sarah and Daniel got down to some serious sea watching. Daniel had worked out that it had been roughly a month since the storm. He estimated that some activity should occur tonight or assuming the parcel took a day to float ashore after the storm it could be the following night, however this was only a calculated guess.

"We had better be prepared and assume it's tonight; I've warned Andy and Bart to keep a special lookout tonight for any movement from the nerd and tomorrow night just in case. Bart will ring me and my boat is ready…" Daniel trailed off.

"What? What's worrying you Daniel?"

"Well you are to be honest, I'm worried that you could get hurt, as we don't know what's out there. I'm worried... I wouldn't be able to live with myself..."

"Daniel, I'm not an ordinary civilian, I know I was injured and left the force but I was trained and worked in one of the country's roughest cities, as you well know and until that prat deliberately crashed our car into poor old Terry, I had never suffered any mishap, so please don't worry and I would worry just as much about you being out there alone."

"OK, you've convinced me, I have no intention of catching anyone single handed, the whole idea is to take photographs of the handover. The actual meeting is just as important as catching anyone. Your mission, should you choose to accept it, [he said in a terrible imitation voice from Mission Impossible] is to take the photographs of the main vessel which will have the nerd on board… And more importantly, the Big Boss!

"All boats as you know have a name and number on the back and the side, it's your job to photograph those, that is the most important thing, and of course as many faces as you can, you know the drill."

They watched all night barely leaving the telescope for a second and as Daniel became a little bleary-eyed with constant staring Sarah would take over. At one stage Sarah had to go out onto the beach with Scamp for his walk and drink in as much fresh air as she could to enable her to stay awake.

However by three o'clock she must have eventually succumbed to dozing off on the sofa, until she felt something blowing her hair and she reached up to stop it only to find the sun was up and it was Daniel holding a cup of what smelled like fresh coffee.

Sarah very gingerly moved to a sitting position as she would not have dreamt she could have fallen asleep on the sofa which was far too soft for her back, but not only that but in the middle of a stakeout!!

"Hi, you poor thing, I left you and fell asleep, I'm sorry." Daniel bent down and kissed her saying he didn't mind and anyway he got to watch her as she slept, contemplating what they would do when they weren't sea watching.

"You're incorrigible Daniel Summers, but I love it."

"I'm going to go now and catch a few hours sleep but first I am going to call in on Bart and Andy, I want to be sure they keep a close eye tonight because if it's going to happen I feel sure it will be tonight."

As Sarah walked Daniel downstairs and out through the shop door a look of pure devilment came over him, taking Sarah in his arms he almost lifted her off her feet with a kiss that was worthy of Rhett Butler in Gone with the Wind. And as he let Sarah up for air he looked discreetly over her shoulder saying.

"I give it about two seconds after I drive away before Alice is hot foot round, to be honest less than two minutes because I just saw her drag Frank behind the counter so that she can dive out of the café before you even have time to shut the door."

"Oh Daniel you are a tease… but I love it and I bet you a pound to a penny you're right, OK leg it and see how long it takes, I'll see you later give me a ring OK?" Sarah said as she gave him a brief kiss on the lips before he dashed across the road to his car. To make it even worse he tooted his horn as he pulled out of the car park.

"I need to know every little detail and you're not letting a single customer in until you tell all." Alice's face was pink with excitement and curiosity, actually she was slightly puffed out where she had hurried unashamedly from the café to Sarah's shop before she had time to shut the door. As Alice looked into Sarah's face she gave a cry of delight.

"Ahah, I can smell it, you and superman were not just sky gazing together and don't kid me because you can't kid a kidder. And who was the guy who left last night with a veritable flea in his ear."

"Alright, have you got time?"

"Don't you worry about me, Frank is minding the café."

"OK, well I'm not opening up yet; I haven't even had my shower or walked Scamp although he did walk himself along the beach at about six am this morning.

"Well the guy who arrived almost giving me apoplexy the other night was someone I used to know, a rather nasty piece of work. Who is now not in the force – he claimed to be a Customs officer and attempted to hoodwink Daniel into thinking he outranked him, but Daniel isn't stupid and checked up on his computer while the slime bag was insulting me. It turns out he is no more than an Assistant Customs man, who thought he was going to walk in on all the work Daniel has done on this drugs bust.

"Anyway Daniel soon sorted him out; to be honest he threatened to throw him out of the window if he came and bothered me again."

"Oh wow, Superman or what… And I won't believe a word of it if you tell me that, his parting kiss this morning wasn't to seal a night of unbridled passion?"

"Oh my God Alice you really must get out more and stop reading so many saucy books." Sarah almost got away with it until Alice came up close to her face and said point blank.

"Look me in the eye… I can tell if a woman is all loved up."
Sarah dropped her gaze and blushed trying again to deflect Alice's suspicions when all of a sudden she couldn't take the pressure any longer. Oh alright you win… yes we have slept together but that

is all I'm going to tell you so don't ask any more!"

"Hah, hah, I knew it, I knew he had eyes for you and I knew you were right for him… I am so good I should run a dating agency."

"Alice in case you have forgotten, you did not introduce us… a parcel of highly dangerous drugs did. You have just put two and two together and hoped it made four that is not a dating agency."

"Now I must have a shower and open my shop I am late as it is, do I have your permission, are you satisfied?"

"Well as I am not going to get any juicy details out of you, I suppose I'll have to be won't I. Will you be seeing him tonight?"

This was said with much innuendo, that Sarah rolled her eyes, saying she was as incorrigible as Daniel.

"Yes he is coming tonight, but we will without doubt be light watching as believe it or not it will be a month since the storm and Daniel feels sure that if something is going to happen it will be tonight. So there will be no hanky-panky so you can give your imagination a rest for this evening I promise. Now can I get showered now please?"

"I'm going, I'm going, see you later." Alice laughed as she eventually left Sarah in peace.

Chapter 20

Sarah walked along the shore with Scamp distractedly picking up shells and rocks, her thoughts a million miles away. It was difficult to think of anything that didn't relate to Daniel, and she suddenly realised how he had crept into her life in every way. She had been so happy since coming to Cockleshell Bay and she couldn't imagine her happiness getting any better and yet it had.

She thought about his wonderful sense of fun, how he made her laugh with his suggestive innuendo. How wonderfully good looking he was, and how he had completely won her parents over with his straight forward honesty and easy going manner. She tried to imagine what her life would be like if Daniel were not in it for any reason.

What would life be like if there weren't any phone calls making arrangements to go on a picnic or have a meal out or even just a drink at her flat? She had thought she was so content and yet now she knew that she never wanted to be without him. Sarah suddenly stopped stock still and said out loud, "I love him!! I love Daniel Summers!"

The day passed in a sort of daze of serene happiness for Sarah, knowing that she was going to spend another night with Daniel. She had to remind herself that the purpose of the night watching was to catch the drug smugglers in the act. While preparing the evening meal her stomach gave the occasional lurch thinking about what was going to happen that night and what could potentially go wrong. One thing she didn't feel was worried, she had total confidence in Daniel but she knew that they both wanted so much to prove the smuggling ring and get some solid evidence; she hoped that she would be good enough to do her part after such along time out of the job.

"Honey I'm home," Daniel shouted as he arrived, coming up the rear stairs to the flat. Sarah's heart gave a leap of excitement at the sheer sight of him. She wondered silently how long that feeling would last or indeed if it would ever go away, she doubted that it would even if they were together years. How could any red blooded woman not react to this gorgeous hunk in his uniform? Especially, when he smiled that smile, and winked his long black eyelashes while placing his muscular arms around her waist and giving it a gentle squeeze, lifting her face for his kiss.

Daniel kissed Sarah's upturned lips, and their hands immediately began searching every contour of each other's body until

Sarah broke away telling him he must eat first. Reminding him how it promised to be a very busy and tiring night and there would be plenty of time for their lovemaking when all this was over. He gave her one last kiss and then as they sat at the table at the window they chatted about their plans for the night.

"Did you talk to Bart and Andy?"

"Yes they will make sure that they ring me if they see the nerd going out this evening, of course I promised that after this was over I would be on what they could think of as an extended holiday and wouldn't be round their yard for a while. Needless to say they were extremely happy.

The boat is ready and I have my camera. It's easy to use, it's digital and doesn't require a flash, are you still alright about this? If you've changed your mind I'll understand."

"I haven't changed my mind; I'm excited it will be strange after such a long time so I'm bound to be a little nervous until I actually get out there but nervous means careful."

Daniel suggested that she put something on that was dark so that she wouldn't be seen in the dark and he insisted she wear a life jacket just in case anything untoward was to happen.

It was a little after two o'clock when Daniel's phone rang and even though they had hoped and even expected it to ring it still made Sarah jump. The lift of Daniel's eyebrows told her it was Bart or Andy which meant the nerd must be launching his dinghy.

Within a few minutes they were out of the flat and into Daniel's vehicle, she had put on her old black police force track suit which she used to wear when she was going to the gym and a pair of plimsolls so that she wouldn't slip or slide in the boat.

Very quickly they were at the dinghy, however before setting out Daniel sent an instant message to the Coastguard and the Customs advising them of his location for surveillance purposes only at the present time, until he let them know of any further changes in the situation.

Then they started out to sea, however as they came within the vicinity of where Daniel thought his outboard would be heard he switched it off and used the oars to get closer. Lights could quite clearly be seen bobbing about and a very small torch beam could also be seen a little distance away. Daniel whispered to

Sarah that he thought the smaller beam would be the nerd's, letting the larger launch know where he was.

As they got closer and closer they could clearly see a large speedboat type, which appeared to have low voltage deck lights. And as the waves bobbed up and down, they also got glimpses of the nerd's little dinghy. Sarah thought to herself he was braver than her to go out in the pitch dark in a fairly choppy sea in such a small boat.

Sarah had her camera at the ready and decided she would take as many photographs as she could and if half of them were no good because of the swell from the sea, surely the other half would be OK, she was pleased Daniel had mentioned that it was waterproof as the splash from the waves was soaking everything, including Sarah.

As she snapped away and Daniel rowed ever closer the name of the Motor Launch which was obviously made for speed, judging by the shape of its hull which became clear enough to get a good shot. As Sarah took the shot she knew it was a good one as she saw quite clearly the name 'Soft Winds' emblazoned on the rear and the side of the launch. She also took clear shots of two people on board the launch quite clearly having a conversation with the nerd.

 Just as she began to feel happy with her mission, from out of nowhere came a massive wave washing over the side of the dinghy and the noise of a loud hailer calling to the large speedboat. The swell from the speeding Launch which she was to find out later was the Customs Launch almost tipped Daniel's boat over and Sarah was thrown unceremoniously onto the floor where she quickly grabbed the first line she could and hung on tight. Daniel threw himself on top of her as the dinghy bobbed around uncontrollably.

They both heard the roar of an engine and knew without a doubt the high speed power boat had disappeared into the night. Daniel however was up in seconds when he had assured himself of Sarah's safety and switched on his overhead powerful searchlights in order to see if the nerd was alright. Knowing his dinghy was no more than a fishing vessel meant for pleasure Daniel knew the guy was likely to drown if he wasn't spotted.

As the swell had calmed slightly when the Customs Launch had gone off in pursuit of the speedboat without a cat in hell's chance of catching it, Sarah managed to pull herself into an upright position so that she could direct the searchlight for Daniel who was frantically searching for the inexperienced nerd. Looking out into a deep black sea in the pitch dark with only the circle of light was worse than looking for a needle in a haystack but Daniel was determined as he knew from Bart and Andy that the chap had no idea how to sail a boat and would most certainly drown.

Just as Daniel was about to switch on his engine so that he could do a sweep of the area he heard a faint voice calling for help. Sarah instantly turned the light towards the sound and there in the deep dark swell of the waves a pale face could be seen. Daniel threw out a life belt for the chap to hang onto but he was clearly too exhausted so Daniel pulled off his trousers and shirt and dived over the side, so far the night had passed without Sarah even thinking about being nervous and yet when Daniel had dived in to save the nerd all Sarah could think of was she wouldn't be able to bear it if anything happened to him.

Daniel though, was a powerful swimmer and before long he had pulled the young man by his chin from behind until they got to the dinghy where he threw the man's arms onto the rope that Sarah had thrown to them. Daniel was fit and agile and had pulled himself back into the dinghy then between the two of them they dragged the half-drowned nerd into the small cockpit of the boat.

It's amazing that when a man is on dry land he looks like a seven stone weakling, but when he is wet he seems to weigh a ton thought Sarah. Before very long Daniel had started the outboard and they were back at the harbour. Bart and Andy were actually very helpful and were aware that something was going on and had a good idea that it had something to do with smuggling and the nerd must be involved somehow, however they certainly never though the nerd would come back half drowned.

They had also seen something going on out on the water where the Customs Launch had advertised their presence with flashing lights enough to wake the dead. Seeing Daniel and Sarah the two lads came over to help pull out the half drowned chap who may have been a smuggler but didn't deserve to drown and sat him up against and old oil barrel.

Within seconds of getting into harbour Daniel was on his phone to Customs to find out who had authorised their launch without his tip off. Sarah had never heard him so angry before as he told whoever it was that their foolhardy behaviour had risked the lives of three people and jeopardised a perfectly executed plan simply because they hadn't followed his instructions to wait for his signal which he would have given and they would have caught the vessel before it had time to take flight.

It was very obvious by the fact that Daniel began to calm down that the other person was making an attempt at an explanation to which Daniel just shook his head. Then all of a sudden the spotlights from another launch could be seen clearly coming into the harbour and slowing down so as to pull closer to the docking area.

Daniel was ready to throttle whoever was responsible for such a massive cock-up. It was as the figure climbed off the launch that both Sarah and Daniel looked in complete and utter dismay at Stevie!!

"What the hell did you think you were doing?" spat Daniel in a barely controlled anger that Sarah had never heard from him before. "Do you realise that you could have killed three people out there tonight simply because you couldn't take instructions?

"I informed the coast guard and the Customs of my intentions and I also informed them that I would give them the green light the minute we had our evidence which was photographs of the exchange and contact between the two vessels.

"Who the hell did you think you were speeding in like something from a Bruce Willis Movie? Nearly drowning the only known member of the gang."

Stevie attempted to bluff out his enormous cock-up by shouting and yelling as he walked towards Daniel. However Daniel, normally a mild mannered and none confrontational kind of guy was fired up because he knew that if things had gone wrong not only could the suspect have been drowned but so could Sarah have been.

He was in Stevie's face in seconds letting him know that he had already spoken to his superiors who had apologised unreservedly to Daniel and had agreed totally that any intervention should have waited until he had tipped them off. Daniel would of course have given them the co-ordinates and the name of the vessel, which would all have been back up with the evidence of the photographs.

Daniel said as calm as he could manage under the circumstances that he wanted Stevie to take the computer nerd to the nearest hospital to be checked out, while he checked to see if the photographs were any good at which point he himself would talk to the Customs office giving them all the information he could.

Stevie blustered and muttered under his breath but he also knew when he was beaten. If it was any other officer who had made such a blunder Sarah would have felt sorry for them, however she had enjoyed every minute of Daniel's dressing down of the pompous prat. She had waited a long time to see Stevie get his comeuppance and how apt that it should be Daniel that was giving it.

Daniel gave a nod to Bart and Andy and reminded them he would be taking a sabbatical for a few months as of tonight and the two men chuckled delightedly. Daniel and Sarah left Stevie to struggle with the exhausted computer nerd back to his launch and no doubt a roasting from his superiors. They climbed back into Daniel's vehicle where only hours before they were contemplating the job and now it was job done and from their point of view as long as the photographs came out, it had been a great success.

Stevie on the other hand would no doubt be in deep water of his own, as Daniel and Sarah had guessed the 'Soft Winds' would be long gone by now. Sarah just hoped that the photos she had taken were sufficient to back up their investigation. Within minutes of linking the camera up with Daniel's onboard computer in his very modern and up-to-date police vehicle clear as a bell could be seen the pictures of the 'Soft Winds' then pictures of the two men from the boat and the computer nerd clearly having an animated discussion, no doubt about the missing package. Sarah had taken multiples of each in case some were a little wobbly, after all it isn't the easiest thing in the world to take photos while the surface is weaving around and bobbing up and down, but these were perfect.

Daniel and Sarah on seeing the images both said in unison with great gusto, "YES!"

And with that they sent copies to the Customs office as promised.

Chapter 21

The first thing both Daniel and Sarah wanted was a hot shower, it may be very warm in the midday sun but in the middle of the night, the ocean was not the place to take a swim. Sarah's shower was a little tight for two, however that became half the fun as Daniel stood behind Sarah with his arms wrapped around her this would be the first time he had actually seen in close proximity the two long scars down her spine where the surgeons had put in the metal rods which by now had knitted her spine together.

He leaned down and kissed the two scars, and if it was within his power to take away the injury then he would do it in a heart beat. As they kissed and soaped each other which aroused their passion they wrapped each other in huge bath sheets before falling into Sarah's bed.

Their lovemaking was torrid; the kind that only those who had experienced near death encounters could understand and as their ardour was at last satiated they lay still gasping in air and wrapped in each others arms. It was the phone that woke Sarah early the next morning, and as she reached out for the receiver and groggily said her number her father quite bright and breezily asked if she was alright as she sounded a little rough?

He said he was ringing to tell her they were coming down later for just the one night and he wondered if anything had happened with Bob and Celia and had she been able to persuade Daniel not to do anything about the card games?

"I told you not to worry Dad; Daniel isn't interested in Bob and Celia's illicit card schools or lock-ins, everything's fine." She said, and she would explain why she was still in bed at eight am in the morning although lots of the population were however Sarah was usually a very early riser.

When Sarah came off the phone Daniel was laughing so much his shoulders were shaking, in fact he had almost stuffed the quilt into his mouth in order not to laugh out loud while she had been on the phone to her father.

She had noticed a sort of squeak but dismissed it but now realised it was Daniel creased with laughter.

"What, what come on tell me what is it?"

"I can't tell you, I can't because if I tell you then you'll feel you should tell your parents and then things will be different and I don't want them to be and neither do they."

"I won't I won't I promise, you've got to tell me now I won't be able to rest until you do, oh come on Daniel tell me please, please."

"Well alright but you must promise me never ever to tell a living soul and that includes Alice this time you can't tell a soul alright?"

"Yes, Yes I promise, just tell me."

"Well you know Bob and Celia?"

"Of course I do now get on with it and stop prevaricating."

"Alright, alright, well did you know that Bob used to run a club in the West End of London which apparently used to employ acts of all different sorts, well being in the city the acts had to be good and interesting from what I hear or they would get booed of the stage.

"Well by all accounts he hired a group of dancers which had come highly recommended but he personally hadn't seen them. It turned out that the dancing group were all… Men in drag!"

At this point Daniel could hardly carry on for laughing especially when watching the expression on Sarah's face.

"Come on, come on you can't stop there!"

"Well the tale goes that after watching the rehearsal Bob had never laughed so much in his life so he hired them. And before long they became a regular booking as they were so good, and the person who made all their bookings was no other than Celia.

"Well apparently Celia and Bob became really good friends, well by all accounts

Bob wanted to deepen the relationship but something seemed to be holding Celia back. Until one night a whole group of drunks came into the club during the act and within minutes the club erupted into a brawl. The drunks said they had come for a spot of gay and drag bashing and they smashed the legs of tables to use as weapons.

"All the regular customers had legged it by this time that left Bob, Celia and a lot of men in drag, gay or otherwise. When Bob tried to pull Celia behind the bar for her own protection, she chose that moment to admit to Bob that she had once been a man called Colin and was strong enough to whack any old drag basher. When Celia looked at Bob's face and saw the shock, the horror, the disbelief then the admiration of a woman/man about to knock the shit out of a room full of drunks in order to protect his friends, Bob himself picked up a baseball bat he kept behind the bar for just such occasions.

"Normally the gender of the dancers Bob would be fighting to protect would be female and not male dressed as female, but to hell all he knew was they were nice people and there was no body going to come into his club and hurt people for no good reason.

"Bob however suffered a fractured skull and woke up in hospital remembering nothing of the table leg that was to have cracked his head wide open. He also suffered a broken collarbone and severe facial bruising where apparently his attacker kept whacking him until he was told Celia smashed chair leg over the drunks head and pole- axed him.

"Celia apparently visited Bob in hospital every day and the men in the ward were under the impression that she was a woman as indeed she was now after three years of gender surgery. They were envious of the attention Celia spent on Bob and thought he was lucky to have such an attentive wife.

"Celia even arranged for the Follies dance troupe to tidy up the club which was in a terrible state and they apparently were very glad to do it for Bob. Eventually when Bob was allowed home he admitted to Celia that even though he knew she had been a man he had never enjoyed anyone's company as much as he did hers and if she felt the same then no one need know any different.

"So that's why they moved to the little village of Cockleshell Bay, and why their secret must remain a secret which has nothing to do with card schools or lock-ins. However can you just imagine what your Mum and Dad would make of that?"

Again Daniel was rolling about in the bed this time Sarah was also in fits of giggles.

"Oh my goodness Dad has always prided himself on his ability to assess people's character, how incredibly wrong can you get?"

"No, no, listen actually his isn't wrong… No he assessed the character of Bob and Celia to be a really nice couple and he was right they are…" Daniel said while attempting to be serious yet not being able to stop laughing.

"It's just that they are not what they seem to be."

"Ha, ha, oh Daniel now I wished I hadn't asked."

"I told you, you wouldn't want to know, because now you know something you don't want to know… Ha ha but listen what does it matter they are a nice couple and what does it matter what she used to be. She is a woman now and that's all you have to think."

"Of all the secrets I have uncovered that takes the cake and I can't even tell Alice."

Daniel pulled Sarah into his arms and saying still with a smile on his face but in all seriousness. "You were wonderful last night."

Sarah laughed at what she thought Daniel was insinuating.

"No you little idiot, out there in the dark; you kept your concentration and took the photographs that will be crucial to the investigation and eventual case against at least one of the smugglers. And if it hadn't been for your ex partner the Coast Guard and the Customs, would have been ready for the launch and had a good chance of catching them."

"Ah well never mind," sighed Sarah, contentedly. "We did our job and solved the mystery of the package. I'll always be grateful for that storm washing the package up on the beach because it brought you to me. I thought I was happy and content even with all Alice's kidding about finding a man washed up on the shore. I wasn't looking for anyone. I didn't think I needed anyone, but now I know I did need someone, and that someone was you and now I can't imagine life without you"

The End

Epilogue

It was on a particularly balmy night in the last day's of the summer after Sarah and Daniel had made soft and passionate love which seemed to get better the more they knew about each other, when Daniel said to Sarah, "Do you ever hear the music; you know you once told me you heard trumpet playing when the wind was in the right direction?"

"No," Replied Sarah. "It's so strange, I miss it. I used to hear it a lot, a haunting tune, like something from a Mexican saloon in an old movie, strange how it just disappeared."

Daniel kissed Sarah's forehead where he had been holding her in his arms as they snuggled in the aftermath of their lovemaking. He slid out of bed and Sarah lay dreamily happy and contented, her eyes closed until a haunting sound came from somewhere in the distance brought Sarah to a sharp sitting position.

The sound was definitely a trumpet and the tune it was playing was 'Oh My Papa' which she remembered very well. She jumped out of bed and pulled on a large t shirt as a nightdress, running to the window and opening it to see standing in the garden in only a pair of boxer shorts was Daniel, playing a bright and shiny trumpet which made the most haunting and wonderful music.

Sarah opened the window whispering, "Daniel Summers, it was you all the time, and it's wonderful!"

"I don't know why you're whispering Sarah, I would imagine the whole village has heard it by now. That's why I play at night and only up on the hill, I had no idea the sound carried so far. Oh did I not tell you I played the bugle in the boy's brigade?"